I0563331

NEKMAN

NEKMAN

Nishant Nalwa

ZORBA BOOKS

Published in India by Zorba Books, 2016

Website: www.zorbabooks.com
Email: info@zorbabooks.com

Copyright © Nishant Nalwa

ISBN Print Book – 978-93-85020-73-5
ISBN eBook – 978-93-85020-74-2

All rights reserved. No part of this book may be reproduced or transmitted in any form or by any means, electronic or mechanical, including photocopying, recording, or by an information storage and retrieval system—except by a reviewer who may quote brief passages in a review to be printed in a magazine, newspaper, or on the Web—without permission in writing from the copyright owner.

Although the author and publisher have made every effort to ensure the accuracy and completeness of information contained in this book, we assume no responsibility for errors, inaccuracies, omissions, or any inconsistencies herein. Any slights on people, places, or organizations are unintentional.

Zorba Books Pvt. Ltd.(opc)

Gurgaon, INDIA

Printed at : Repro Knowledgecast Limited, Thane

Dedicated to Sai Baba

Acknowledgment

The biggest boon on this earth is Mother who love you selflessly, hereby firstly I would like to thank my Mother Mrs. Mamta Nalwa, who has taught me the values of life and who has craved my personality. My mother has given me the best out of best in life whether it was my school, college or for a matter of fact my clothes.

I would like to thank my father Mr. Brajesh Nalwa for providing me whatever whenever I asked, compromising on his own wishes. I also thank to my brother Jai Nalwa who is like a son to me and a trust which will always be with me throughout my life.

Life gets changed when someone goes out of your life and also when someone steps-in your life. Quoting this I would like to thank someone who stepped in my life, my lady luck and love of my life Swarnali Nalwa who loves me till the moon and back. She stood by my dream and helped me in all aspects to launch my dream, 'NEKMAN'. "I love you my sweetheart, you are my everything".

Also, would like to thanks my extended families, my In-laws Mrs. Manika Biswas and Mr. Samiran Biswas and my maternal uncle aunty Mrs. Bakul Choudhary and Mr. Naveen Choudhary for all their love and affection toward me.

Thank you to Mrs. Abha Rani Singh my aunt, who is a great source of inspiration to me and from whom I learnt how to face and deal with challenges of life.

A special thanks to Saikat Dey who sketched cover page of my book.

Thank you my Grand Mother Mrs. Kanta Choudhary for all her blessings and my cute cousins Kirti & Hritik.

Last but not the least I would like to thank my close friends Arpit, Sundeep, Kapil, Manvi, Shantunu, Aakarsh, Ankit, Siddharth & Vishant to make my life worthwhile. You guys Rock!

Thank you so much my editor for polishing my book and providing me valuable feedback.

A Big thanks to my publisher **Zorba Books** to make my Dream **"NEKMAN"** into a reality.

Content

Prologue

A kind hearted person – yes, this is the meaning of my name 'NEKMAN'.

I am in a good mood reading the daily newspaper in my lavish lawn while sipping my favorite Twining's tea. I am the proud owner of one of the biggest bungalows on Delhi's Golf Course road - beyond anything I have ever dreamt of in life.

According to me, the most powerful thing in this world is time - which can make or break anyone's fortune. I always respect time, especially after going through bad times that almost destroyed me completely.

It was 7:30 am according to my Rolex. I'm sure any other watch in the world would have told me the same, but, through the crown of a Rolex, you see the same time but at a different angle. Success is all yours if you can also make someone see something at a different angle.

I never thought, while going through my bad phase, that one day I would be sitting so peacefully, with no worries. The kind of life I am now living, is almost a miracle, though it did take hard work as well. Nothing comes without effort and destiny also plays a part - luck alone, is like a body without soul.

"Sir, which car you would like take today?" one of my drivers asked.

"Whichever you want to drive today," I said with a smile on my face.

When you have eight luxury cars in your garage, you can select your drive according to mood.

"Sarita, can you please bring me the invitation which I received yesterday?" I asked one of my staff. We were a family of five and I had five permanent staff in residence.

"Sure sir."

I opened the invite and scanned it from top to bottom. The last words on the invite were: "With Love…" I smiled looking at the word 'Love' which had played a big role in changing my destiny.

I got ready to leave for work and took the invitation along – it was an invitation to be interviewed in a popular television show, on my journey from the past to the present.

Just 15 minutes from office, a traffic inspector stopped my car.

"Hey what happened?" I asked my driver. I had been reading a newspaper in the back seat.

"Don't know sir." He got out of the car and headed towards the policeman.

Five minutes later, my driver was still arguing with the inspector and seemed to be getting nowhere. Finally I stepped out of my car to have a word.

"What is the problem inspector?" I asked, coming up from behind.

He turned toward me and said: "You need to pay a fine of 2000 rupees for over-speeding." In a fraction of a second, recognition flashed in our eyes. Eleven years ago, the same inspector had handcuffed me, slapped me and tortured me in jail for a night. That too for a crime I had not committed!

"Ah! Nekman," the inspector said.

"Yes, it's me. How come you have shifted to the traffic department?" Eleven years ago he used to be the SHO (Station House Officer) of South Delhi area and in these eleven years, he should have grown tremendously, especially considering the way he used to take bribes.

"I got demoted after getting caught in a few bribery cases," he admitted.

"Everyone has to pay for his bad karma."

He looked at me for a second, then apologized.

"Today I am in a position where I can make your life miserable and put you out of your uniform, but I am not going to. No need to say sorry to me – in fact it's good to see you doing your duty."

I paid the spot fine and we continued heading towards my office.

"Sir, we have reached office," my driver said.

I was in deep thought, meeting that inspector had triggered a flashback.

"Excuse me sir, we have reached office," my driver said again, recalling me to the present.

I was about to step out of my car but didn't. Instead, I asked the driver to give me the car keys.

"What happened sir? You want to go somewhere else? I can take you."

"No, thanks. I will go myself."

I took the keys and started the car. The theme of the upcoming interview and the meeting with the inspector was sending me on a journey into the past, because of which I was in no mood for work.

"Excuse me, can I have a quarter of rum?" I asked the vendor as I reached a liquor shop.

Looking at me the vendor said, "One hundred and ten rupees."

After that I went to a grocery store and picked up a packet of chocolate cookies.

Everything had changed in these eleven years but the price of rum had hardly jumped from what it had been and the same brand of chocolate cookies was still available.

With the rum and chocolate cookies for company, I went for a long drive because I always connect life to a road – a road with many red lights, speed breakers, twists and turns. To be a good driver you have to get past it all and keep going.

Life too, is filled with twist and turns, highs and lows, love and hate and through it all you still need to keep going. Fear is a dead end; one should always keep moving forward in the road of life.

I took rum, not to drink, but to remember what I was like eleven years back...

1

The Un-fresh Start

It was all over. I was in trauma after my engagement had been called off. I think any human being in this world, would be in the same frame of mind that I was in, after suffering such a set-back.

"Nekman, please wake up. You're getting late for office!" Mom shouted.

"Okay mom," I mumbled.

She came to my room with incense sticks, a part of her daily prayer ritual. "Seriously, whatever happens, happens for good. You are safe my boy, and you are going to find a very beautiful girl," she said, kissing my forehead.

In my mind I wondered: What was the definition of beautiful? A person who was good looking, a person who had pure thoughts, a person of wise words, or a person who could be trusted? Well, whatever the definition, I cared a damn. Because for me, the word 'beautiful' was all spurious. I couldn't tell if Hinsa, my ex fiancé, was a beauty or a beast. Did she have a heart of gold or a heart of coal? After the crappy stuff that happened recently, it was surely of coal!

Fifteen days had passed since her family had called off our engagement and returned the rings. Her father, a pure Punjabi smart ass, had registered in court, a legal document stating that the engagement had been called off with the mutual consent of both families, though my family had no wish to call it off. Somehow, being working class, with no power or influence, you had to follow the diktat of the more powerful party in front of you. Yes, Hinsa was from a business family. Although her father's business was in debt, her family, including her four brothers, enjoyed good status, and the rest of her relatives too, were quite influential and well off.

"Nekman!!" Mom shouted again as I was just stepping out of the shower. "Son, your breakfast is ready, please come soon."

"Coming..." I mumbled in a dull, lifeless voice. Anyone listening to me would have assumed from my tone that these were the last words of a person departing this kind universe.

"Has dad left for work?" I asked at breakfast.

"Yes," mom said.

"I could have dropped him off at the Metro."

"He was getting late and you know he always walks to the Metro to save fuel, which is 71 rupees per liter at present."

"Mom, why does he behave like this?"

"What do you mean? He wants to save money for our family that's why he makes these sacrifices."

"But of what use are these small savings? Did it help when my engagement was called off?"

"It's all destiny my son, leave it to God," mom said quietly.

At times I felt guilty that I traveled by car while dad took the Metro. Unfortunately I was not able to persuade him to take the car as my elephant-like sedan guzzled 8 kmpl. Let's not go into why I forced my father to buy this car in the first place. My choice of car, at that time, was influenced by my ex fiancé Hinsa Dogra, whose name, by the way, was an exact match for her personality – it was the Hindi word for violence.

My father was a man of his word – a typical, 9-6 working class man, who had come up the hard way. He knew the importance of money - that's why at the age of 56 he was still working hard and trying to save. Somewhere, deep down, even I realized the importance of money – especially as the major reason my engagement had been called off was "the money, honey".

"I have prepared rajma rice for your lunch today," mom said. My mom is a typical Punjabi mother whose main mission is to cook day and night and feed the family, and I am a typical Punjabi son, always turning to mother for food.

"Something very good is going to happen, I was reading Sai Geeta and got a very good answer from it regarding your marriage," mom said.

Mom was a great disciple of Sai Baba. Sometimes I wondered how anyone could have this kind of direct connection with God as mom seemed to have. She was so sure that something good was going to happen, even while nothing was going right - but hats off to mom's devotion.

"Yeah, sure!" I mumbled sarcastically.

"Why are you so irritated?" mom asked.

It's just two weeks since my three-year relationship has been called off, I'm entitled to feel irritated, I thought. At that time I was in a kind of depression. I couldn't bear to be questioned and keeping quiet was the best reply.

"Mom I am leaving for work," I said.

"Bye son, don't forget to bow your head in front of Sai Baba and apply vibhuti (holy ash) as you leave." It was a rule in our house to apply Sai Baba's vibhuti before leaving for the day and I used to have some faith in that.

2

Office Office

"Hey dude, Wassup? Looking cool today," - that was my boss, Suraj.

"All good...and you?"

"Your honeymoon period is almost over Nekman, 3 months are up, now pull up your socks and start learning new technologies."

"Yes sir, sure I will," I said.

"Great!" Suraj headed back to his cubicle.

It was like an alien planet to me, everywhere technology.

I had never thought in my wildest dreams that I would end up working for an IT company – a decision taken for Hina's sake. I had always wanted to become an actor, a superstar, but landed up here instead. Such is life! But I still had hopes that someday I would crack an audition and would sit next to Aamir and Salman Khan in Bollywood.

"Look, I have something for you," my colleague Sonupriya said. She was the most intelligent and charismatic candidate in our batch - the one who got the Best Presenter award from the management during our induction period.

"What?" I asked.

She gave me two chocolates and said that all would be well soon.

I smiled and thanked her. We hardly knew each other, an acquaintance of only three months, but she was the only person in whole office with whom I had shared that my engagement had been called off.

"Come on, let's go for a cup of tea," she said.

"No thank you." I opened up my laptop.

"Nekman, don't worry, you are a great guy," she walked to her seat.

At 2 pm, all my colleagues came back from lunch and one of them asked me why I wasn't joining them for lunch these days.

"No reason... I just wasn't hungry, that's why I didn't join you guys," I said.

"But every day you say that you're not hungry."

"Don't get me wrong but I haven't been well the last few days that's why I'm skipping lunch," I said.

"Okay, do as you wish."

In the corporate world you don't have friends. It's the truth. Offices are for work, not friendships. Just to be polite, people ask about you and your life. They don't really want to delve deep. All they want is a 'corporate relationship'.

By 7 pm all my colleagues had left for home. I was the only person from the new batch still at my table and believe me, I had done nothing since morning. I was just sitting in front of computer physically while my mind was wandering elsewhere, thanks to Hinsa. I was reeling from a double blow: a job that I was not at all happy with and deserted by one whom I had hoped would be my better half in the near future.

My boss, while leaving office, saw me sitting at my desk till late. He came towards me and asked me if everything was alright.

"You seem a little disturbed these past few days?"

"Yes sir, I am a little disturbed."

"Why? What happened?"

"Sir, my engagement's been called off."

"Oh God! This is seriously bad news," Suraj said.

"Yes sir."

"But you know what Nekman? A similar thing happened to my younger brother. The girl with whom we were planning his marriage was involved with a number of men, which we came to know only after the engagement. We had to call it off. You are safe now. Imagine if the girl would have done something wrong after your wedding, then it would be more painful for you."

"Right Suraj," I replied but somewhere I thought: "I'm sick of these fucking consolations – 'everything is good, you are safe, good this happened right now, blah'."

"But don't mix your personal life with professional life. Work hard, okay?"

"Yes Suraj," I said and wondered why the hell I shared my situation with him. Ultimately he had reverted to corporate speak – reminding me very smartly, not to mix professional and personal life.

I was not able to accept Suraj's advice - how can one concentrate on professional work when one's personal life is all fucked up?

My boss is a good person to work with, perhaps I was wrong to expect something more from him.

"Hey Nekman, I have marked you in mail with our vendor, please follow through," Suraj said and left.

I had just finished reading the relevant mail when my phone started ringing.

The Caller ID flashed 'Surjeet' and I was sure he must have been on a Con-call with Arvind. Surjeet and Arvind were my two best buddies and the only positives in my life at that time.

"Hello?"

"Nekman, my brother," it was Arvind. I was right about the Con-call.

"Chak de!! Cheers!! So dudes, where are we having drinks tonight?" Surjeet was upbeat.

"Wherever my brother Nekman chooses," Arvind said.

"So, shall we go to Gurgaon?" Surjeet said.

"Stop bro. I am not in a mood to go anywhere tonight. You people carry on," I said

My friends were well aware of my situation, that's why every fortnight they planned parties to cheer me up.

"Its medicine bro, medicine!" Surjeet said.

For Surjeet alcohol was the best medicine for any kind of pain in this world. He used to drink a lot and made others drunk as well.

"Seriously, I am not in a mood to go anywhere," I said.

"Come on bro, this is not done. Today there is a zombie party in Gurgaon with lots of killer, sexy zombie girls," Arvind said.

"Yippee!" Surjeet screamed over the phone. "Be ready, we are going to pick you up in 30 minutes."

When girls and booze, plus your partners-in-crime are going to be with you, then whatever your situation is, you are going to give it a second thought before turning it down.

"Okay brothers, I will meet you at 9 pm but we must get back by 12 am max," I said.

"Okay coming, cheers!!" Arvind and Surjeet hung up.

By 9:15 pm Arvind and Surjeet drove up to my office; I was standing at a tea shop nearby.

"Dudes both of you are insane - with such a loud music in the car you are standing right outside my office gate! I have told you so many times, always come to Papu's tea shop, 200 meters ahead. I am there right now, come quickly if you people don't want me to see with a pink slip soon in my hand," I said.

"Chill bro, we're coming," Arvind said. Both of them giggled and hung up.

I climbed into the back seat. The first thing I saw was that Arvind's and Surjeet's glasses were filled and my 100 Pipers quarter was lying on the seat.

100 Pipers was our favorite drink. It was quite expensive but we could afford it as all three of us were earning.

"Nekman bro, start with your quarter, man," Surjeet said.

I poured 10 ml to Bhairo Baba, God of alcohol. India is a country full of gods; there are gods for every occasion in India, love, sex or drink - and we liked to start by dedicating a peg to Bhairo Baba.

"Cheers," we said after I had poured my peg and we started for Gurgaon.

"Give me some ice," Surjeet said.

"No more ice for you. We are left with less than half a packet," Arvind said.

Arvind was very calculative about everything and used to get tense over petty things as well - as if there was about to be an income tax raid on his home, where he would have to account for all expenditure.

"I will buy some more at Gurgaon. Give me the ice packet you asshole," Surjeet said.

"Okay but only one cube," Arvind said.

I was drinking my peg but not really enjoying it as my mind was elsewhere.

"What the hell you are thinking about?" Surjeet directed the question at me.

"Nothing"

"Please tell us Nekman. From the time you got into the car, you've been silent," Arvind said.

"Nothing", I said again, but this time in a dull voice.

"Okay fine, give me your glass. Let me pour another peg for you," Arvind said.

I gave him my glass at once; my mind was in turmoil thanks to Hinsa and alcohol was the only thing I knew off to take mind off things. "Make it a large," I said.

"Make my kind of peg for Nekman," Surjeet said magnanimously, turning up the volume.

We reached the zombie party. It was packed with super sexy girls in backless dresses, flaunting their legs and cleavage. All the girls were damn hot and just one step away from being naked.

Our eyes glittered at the sight. Suddenly I realized I was feeling great. Standing amongst the world's most amazing hot chicks, I forgot all my sorrows and began enjoying myself. Watching me drool over the girls, Surjeet and Arvind exchanged a wicked smile.

I was 8 pegs down and it was 12:30 at night. Even Arvind and Surjeet were completely drunk.

Surjeet was the DOD (devil of drinks) among us, because after 12 pegs he was the only one who could still drive safely. We were on our way back from that crazy party and all went well.

We were happy to cross the Gurgaon toll safely. To our luck there were no police at the toll with Breathalyzers.

"Why has God has done this to me?" I burst out.

After a minute of silence, Surjeet said: "I didn't get you."

"Why was my engagement called off? Why is God punishing me?" I agonized.

"Bro leave it, everything will be all right. It'll be all good. Don't worry," Arvind said.

"What good will happen? Everything is fucked up for me and she is enjoying life," I raved.

"Why the hell are you talking like a loser? You have everything going for you - loving parents, good job... and how do you know she is enjoying life?" Surjeet said.

"I know because it's been 15 days and Hinsa hasn't called me once. I know she will find someone even better soon. God is against me," I said bitterly.

"Are you mad? Why would God hate you? Hinsa and her family are wrong and they are the ones who have messed up. Don't you worry," Arvind said.

"Arvind is right, believe me you will find someone special very soon. She is not going to find anyone better than you; just wait and watch," Surjeet said.

Surjeet played our favorite Punjabi soundtracks and I began to felt better with all the positive reinforcement coming my way.

That night I slept well.

―――――∽∾――――

3

Another Day

"Good morning ladies and gentlemen, welcome to the Cisco Summit for data center virtualization."

Being an employee of the 4th largest IT Company in India was something to be proud off – also, I got to attend a number of events with the world biggest information technology vendors. Cisco was one of them.

"Ladies and gentlemen we are going to start the session - questions will be taken at the end, once all sessions are over," Cisco's presenter said.

All attendees nodded their head, including me.

Sitting in 7 star hotels feted with good food, drinks and expensive gifts from the vendors was the only motivation for me to attend these sessions and believe me, throughout my career, I had not missed a single event.

"Hey, you know only 10 days are left for our review," a colleague whispered.

"Okay good," I said.

"You know our first appraisal totally depends upon our review. Be prepared buddy."

Compared to the other big trauma in my life, I thought goofing up a review was not such a big deal. So I spent my time at the event trying to access Hinsa's Facebook page. But she had blocked me out and blocked out my whole family and all our common friends.

"Ladies and gentlemen, let's break for tea and continue the session in fifteen minutes," the presenter announced. I realized that half the session was over and I was still obsessing over Hinsa's Facebook page.

I went out of the conference room and called Arvind.

"How are you bro?"

"All good - just little sore throat from the icy pegs," Arvind said.

"Okay, take care. I'll see you in evening," I said.

The moment I hung up, an unknown number flashed on my phone. My heart started racing and I ran outside to the hotel reception.

"Hello?" I uttered, nervously. "Hello?"

"I love you..." She was crying on phone, yes, it was my ex fiancée Hinsa.

"Hinsa?"

"I love you Nekman, I love you. My parents did it. It was not my idea," she sobbed.

"Just tell me one thing," I said.

"What?"

"Do you still love me and want to marry me?"

"Yes."

"Then, let's run away together," I said.

"No."

"Why not?"

"I can't leave my parents and see them crying anymore because of me… it's enough Nekman," she said.

"You love me and I love you, then where's the problem? Why can't you leave your parents?" I asked.

"I really don't have any answer for that."

"Fine, but why the hell, did your parents do this? Can you answer that at least?"

"You know very well why, Nekman. It's because our horoscopes don't match."

"Wow! Nice joke. If you remember, both our parents went to the astrologer and showed our horoscopes well before our engagement. At that time there was no issue, then why now?" I argued.

"We were both quarrelling constantly after the engagement, so my parents went to a different astrologer who told them that both of us were not good for each other. The astrologer also said that if we did marry, our future would be bleak and it would end in divorce."

This was bullshit. She wasn't giving me the real reason.

"Unofficially we've been married for the past three years. Think about it - I have seen you as my wife, my better half and now..." my voice broke.

"Sorry Nekman, I cannot simply abandon my parents... goodbye, take care," she said.

"Wait! We can work out something," I said desperately.

"Sorry Nekman. Nothing can be done now," she said firmly. "Nekman, bye!"

She hung up.

I was in shock for five minutes, then I marveled at how drastically a person could change. What a fool I had been to trust her.

The same Hinsa who was now declaring that she could not see tears in eyes of her parents, had, three years earlier, cried on my shoulder that she would never forgive her dad for giving her a hard time throughout her childhood and she how she hated her mom for treating her like a maid.

I also recall her telling me that I was everything to her – more precious than her father or mother; the best thing to happen in her life. Was it all crap?

We had spent the past three years like husband and wife. I had never thought in my wildest dream that this could happen someday; that she could react this way.

I left the conference that very moment. One thing was still unclear to me - the real reason for our break up. I was not going to swallow the story that our engagement was called off because of our horoscopes.

I went to the Sai Baba temple and sat there till I calmed down. Then I called Surjeet.

"Nekman, wassup? How's the conference going?"

"Did not attend," I said.

"Why? What happened? Are you alright?"

"Yes. What could happen to me?"

"Wait, Arvind is calling. Let me put him on conference."

"Hey guys, wassup? I have a surprise for you," Arvind said.

"What?" we asked.

"My car got delivered today. Yippee!"

"Hey, congrats bro!"

"So, where is the party Arvind?" Surjeet asked.

"Yes dude. Where is the party?"

"Today 9 pm sharp, we are meeting and the rest is a surprise," Arvind said.

"Cheers!!" Surjeet screamed.

I didn't tell them about my conversation with Hinsa. Arvind was excited about his new car and I didn't want to spoil his mood.

"The AC in this car is damn good, it chills like the Himalayas," Arvind said.

"Take your quarter Nekman," Surjeet said.

"Yup. Give it to me," I said.

Arvind's new car was our new car bar, previously Surjeet car was our car bar.

"Bro where is your peg?" I asked Arvind.

"I am not drinking. My dad will kill me," Arvind said.

"Why what happened?" I asked.

"Heheheheh," Surjeet giggled. "Arvind's father has given him notice that if Arvind is ever caught drunk again in life, then he will be kicked out of the house and his father will go on a pilgrimage forever, giving the whole business away to charity," Surjeet said and laughed his ass off.

Listening to Surjeet's comment even I laughed out aloud. Arvind looked like he wanted to beat us both up. I signaled to Surjeet that Arvind was embarrassed and we quickly controlled our giggles.

Obviously his father would threaten this. What can one expect from a man who is strictly religious and above all, a follower of Jainism. Arvind was a Jain - his father had never tasted a sip of alcohol in his life, whereas Arvind was a big time drunkard.

"Very funny!!" Arvind responded to Surjeet's comment and our suppressed laughter.

After a minute's pause, Surjeet and I broke out laughing again at the hilarious thought of Arvind's father donating the whole business to charity if Arvind was ever caught drunk again.

The best thing about friends is that whatever is the situation, or to whatever extent you are feeling down, you forget everything the moment when you are with them. I was crying in the afternoon and now, with them, I forgot all my worries. As I mentioned earlier, these two people were the only positives in my lives at that time.

4

D-Day

10:30 am. I was late to work and it was D- day. The day of my first review.

Every day was same to me as I was emotionally disturbed. Every second day I used to go for drinks with my friends. They also used to drink with me, but the difference was, my friends use to drink for gain and I use to drink in pain.

I didn't even realized that the day of my review had arrived. Our Director was ready to give left, right, up and down to all management trainees. Deep down I knew I would not be one of the chosen, because my Director was going to tear his hair and hand me a pink slip after reviewing my performance of the past four months.

"Hey dude how was your review?" I asked a colleague.

"Fantastic! Masky was very happy with my performance and he told me that next month he will recommend my name for an IBM conference outside India," he said.

"Good."

"Go in, it's your turn. Masky told me to send you to his cabin," he said

I was not able to think of anything as my mind was in turmoil. Although it was now a month since my engagement had been called off, I was still not over it. I decided to assume the pose of statue. I would sit and listen to whatever he said, well, I knew he would just not say anything, instead he would shout it!

"Good morning sir. May I come in?" I asked.

"Yes Nekman, come inside."

"Thank you sir," I said and sat down.

The table between us was neat and clean with all files well arranged in his cabin. Nothing was out of place, which showed how well organized he was. There were two separate ultra-bright lights in his cabin, which, as all we management trainees knew, had been set up on Masky's recommendation, as he wanted his room to be full of positive vibes.

Then I saw two posters - one of Lord Jesus and another of Bill Gates who is known as the God of Information Technology. There was also a family photograph on his desk with his wife and kid. Everything was arranged so perfectly that the room looked more like a movie set rather than a real life Director's cabin.

"So how has your journey in HCL Technologies been so far?" Masky asked.

"Good sir. Very good."

"Great. So what have you learnt in the past few months?"

I went blank and did not utter a word.

"What have you learnt in the past few months?" he asked again.

"Okay sir. Good sir," I mumbled nervously.

He looked at me for two minutes as his questions and my answers were totally at variance, like North Pole and South Pole.

"Nekman are you alright?" He asked.

I didn't answer.

He shook my hand. "Nekman are you alright?" he asked again.

I shivered and said, "Yes sir."

Suddenly I came to my senses and realized that I was in the first review of my life.

"Nekman, is everything fine?" he asked patiently.

"No sir," I said.

"What happened? Why you are so disturbed?" He asked.

"My engagement got called off last month."

"Is your reporting manger aware of this?"

"Yes sir."

He was silent for two minutes.

"I am so sorry," he said.

"Don't be sir."

"So are you happy with your current role or you want a role change?" he asked.

He had understood my feelings. Rather than go in for a review he started asking me things which could make me comfortable and divert my mind.

"No sir, I am happy with my role. But as I am not from a technical background, my graduation is in commerce and after that an MBA in marketing, I need more time to understand the process of the IT industry," I said. (Though in truth, I was hardly making an effort to understand it.)

"Okay. So how much time more do you need to understand the whole process and working of our organization?" he asked.

"Two months," I said confidently.

"Done. I grant you two more months. Learn and come again for a review," he said.

"One more thing sir."

"Tell me."

"Sir, since you asked about the role change, at present I am okay with my current role, but in future I want to see myself working on the branding for HCL Technologies," I said.

"Hmm, I will look into it."

"Thank you sir."

"Nekman, life is not full of choices, what you get - respect that, leave the rest to destiny and God."

Four hours later, I was having coffee in the cafeteria and ruminating over the last thing Masky had told me: "life is not full of choices…" I don't know whether he was speaking from experience in his personal life or corporate life, but something in what he said resonated with me and I took it as a learning for my life.

Another thing I realized was that he was not the tyrant that people made him out to be. This was another learning for me – never to blindly believe or rely on other people's perceptions.

It was 8:30 pm when I returned from office. Dad was in his room watching TV and mom was cooking. Joy, my younger brother was playing an online game in his room as he was not allowed to play outdoors. He was in grade 12 and the all-important board exams were around the corner. Joy use to study for hours. Sometimes I felt that his studies too suffered due to my engagement drama.

"Hey brother," Joy said as I entered his room.

"Hi dude. How're your studies going?"

"Okay types."

"Oh! Concentrate more, champ."

"Yes, doing that only."

"But you are playing games on the laptop instead of studying. Shall I tell mom?"

"No please!"

"Okay five minutes, then you'd better hit the books, bro."

"Nekman..." mom called me. "How was your review?"

"Not good."

"Why what happened?"

"Nothing, just..." I shrugged.

"Son, do concentrate on your job and perform well otherwise it will be very difficult to carry on, there is so much of competition in the industry," she said.

"I know mom," I said.

"I have bought all the puja material for tomorrow, except for flowers and incense sticks which you have to get right now."

This was a new trend in Delhi. "Ganpati Visarjan" is an important festival in Mumbai but as Delhi is number one in showing off, Delhi people had begun celebrating it on a larger scale. Another reason why Delhi people started Ganpati Visarjan was their excess, unaccounted money which they wanted to splash any which way.

My mother was one of those religious women who fasted for three days so that some prosperity and enlightenment would touch my family and dispel the negative energies surrounding us.

5

Ganpati Baapa Moriya

"Ganpati baapa moriya mangal murti moriya," all of us raised our voices in unison as we finished the puja at my home. We had invited some of my relatives and by default Surjeet and Arvind were there helping with the puja arrangements. My mom had made delicious homemade 'modak', a sweet offered to Lord Ganesha as modaks are believe to be his favorite dish.

"Nekman come here and bow your head," mom called me.

"Go Nekman, go," Arvind giggled.

"Coming mom," I said.

"Ask your friends also to come," mom said.

"Call them yourself."

"Surjeet, Arvind...come here!" mom shouted from puja room.

"Coming aunty." There was no escaping mom.

"Bow your head with Nekman," mom commanded both of them.

"Yes aunty," they said obediently.

"How you are Surjeet and Arvind? How is everyone in your family?"

"All good."

"Lord Ganesha has protected you Nekman," my mother said.

"Mom, stop it."

"Nekman, this is the truth. It is good that fool went out of your life." Mom was referring to Hinsa.

"Okay fine. Now stop it mom," I said.

"You tell me Surjeet, what sort of girl will not stand up for her love and above all betray her love?" mom was on her favorite topic.

"Yes aunty. She was wrong. Arvind and I have been telling Nekman again and again to stop thinking about her. There are millions of girls in this world; it's is not end of life," Surjeet said.

"I've even deleted her old messages and photographs from Nekman's phone," Arvind said.

"See, your friends are so supportive. Be happy Nekman. There is no point thinking about her. Above all you are blessed with such good friends. You should cherish what you have."

"Yes mom I know," I mumbled.

Sometimes, when you are wounded, the pain cannot be understood by anyone in the world – friends or family, however close. Yes, to an extent they can share your feelings, but in the end, you are the only one who knows the depth of that pain.

Your friends and family can support you and try to alleviate the pain but you also need to put in the effort, so you can be happy.

"Ganpati baapa moriya mangal murti moriya." We went to the Yamuna River in Delhi for Visarjan as there is no sea, like there is in Mumbai. We all raised our voice once again and completed the Visarjan on a positive note.

"Nekman son you are protected…" Arvind mimicked my mom perfectly and both Surjeet and Arvind fell around laughing.

"Very funny, right?" I said.

"No Nekman. It's not funny you are protected," Surjeet said and again both of them giggled.

"Drink your beer, don't annoy me," I said.

Yes, we were drinking at night after Ganpati Visarjan. My parents were very tired and slept early, giving me the opportunity to escape from my home with the help of my younger brother. I asked him to keep his phone near his pillow so that, without ringing the house bell, I could re-enter the house late at night.

Arvind's parents were out of station attending some marriage and for Surjeet, being out late was never a problem.

"Cool Nekman cool, just kidding man," Arvind said.

"You know what Nekman? Even I am unhappy within," Surjeet confided.

"What? Why?"

"Don't know, I mean I want to do something," Surjeet said.

"You are handling your construction business brother, what more can you want? You are making good money from this business too."

"No you don't understand." Surjeet drained his second bottle.

"Tell me."

"I want to do something on my own - not just run dad's business. I want to create my own identity."

"Yes, even I want the same Surjeet," Arvind said, taking a long sip from the bottle.

"Guys, you've completed your MBA, that too from London. Both of you have seen the world, now you two are talking like losers; please give me a break," I said.

"Do you know I was earning 1 lakh rupees a month in London? Now I just go to my dad's college and sit on the golden chair he has given me, nothing more," Arvind said.

"I am trying to understand you guys, that's why I am saying we are MBA grads. If you're not satisfied with your work or you want to have your own identity then start thinking in that direction. Make a business plan, find investors, or else if you want to go for a job, do it. There's no one stopping you. You guys have to take a stand and initiate it. Even I am not satisfied with my job. I want to do something creative in my life; I am certainly not going to be in the I.T. industry forever. I will definitely make a move sooner or later. If I also start thinking like you two, then I won't be able to live – as it is my love life is crap and even my job is heading in the same direction." I completed my motivational speech.

They both looked at me and nodded their head solemnly.

"So let's take an oath," I said.

"What oath? Who has been selected PM among us?" Arvind said and we all laughed.

"No I'm serious. From now on all three of us will concentrate on our careers."

"Okay, but don't forget it applies to you also. And on the personal front you should not be emotionally disturbed, just remove that girl from your mind," Surjeet said.

I didn't answer.

"Hey Nekman, say something," Arvind said.

"Okay guys, I'm in".

"Yippee!" we all shouted and finished our third bottle of beer.

"But…" Arvind said.

"But, what?"

"Before we all start implementing what we have decided, let's take a good break somewhere far, to regenerate ourselves. What say guys?" Arvind asked.

"London! Let's go London, the Queen's land," Surjeet said.

"Yes, even I miss London very much Surjeet," Arvind said.

"Are you guys serious? London?" I asked.

"Yes," they both replied.

"But…" I said.

"Nekman brother, no if's and but's please, we agreed to your oath now you have to agree to our plan as well," Arvind said.

"Yes Nekman come on! We are going, that's it," Surjeet said.

"But…"

"No BUT again, we are going," both of them roared. Well, I thought, my motivational speech for their benefit is ending up costing me a hefty amount. On the other hand, there was no need for me to continue saving as I had become single again and was not planning to mingle or get married in the near future.

"Okay, let's rock London!" I said.

"Yippee…" The three of us screamed as we drained our fourth Bud.

London Diaries

Heathrow airport London. It was an amazing experience to be landing in Queen's Country where the airport itself seemed like a monument. We came out hunting for a cab.

London was in front of my eyes, I cannot express how I felt at that moment. It was like a fairyland, the roads so clean and clear as if they had never been kissed by a tyre. They looked virginal. The weather was so pleasant that surely no one could lose their temper here, unlike in India. The most attractive sight to my eyes, were the hot chicks of London - each and every girl looked like a model; a film star. All girls were snow white in color and they were just mouthwatering! I didn't want to blink even for a second and miss viewing the eye candy. It was as if God has blessed London with an endless number of the most beautiful girls in the whole universe.

"Sir, where would you like to go?" A young and beautiful Snow White was addressing us.

I was astonished to see a girl cab driver that too one who looked like fashion model. In India, due to gender discrimination, you hardly see ladies taking up this kind of work.

Surjeet gave her a street name and she came with her cab. I quickly jumped into the front seat to grab the opportunity to interact with that beautiful girl.

"Hello," I said.

"Hello," the cab driver replied.

"What is your name?" I asked.

Arvind laughed looking outside window.

"Silvana," she said.

"Great! Are you British?"

"No sir, I'm from Romania," she said," Is this your first visit to London?"

Surjeet was about to reply but Arvind quickly interrupted. "Yes, it's our first time in the UK."

I looked enquiringly at Arvind. Why was he was lying? Arvind indicated that I should remain silent.

Surjeet kicked Arvind.

"Hey Silvana, can you guide us around London?" Arvind asked.

"Yes Silvana, please help us explore London!" She seemed taken aback by my excitement.

"Actually we are here for the first time and only for 7 days so can you be our guide for a single day?" I asked.

"Yes, only for a day Silvana, if you are okay with that," Arvind said.

"Sure guys, I will join you tomorrow morning and help you explore London."

"Thanks Silvana." Both Arvind and I chatted continuously with Silvana on the way to our hotel.

"So shall I pick you from here again?" she asked.

"From where?" I asked.

"Sir, we have reached your destination," she replied.

Suddenly Arvind and I realized that we indeed reached to our hotel and Surjeet was taking the bags from the cab boot.

"Oh, thank you. Thank you so much, you are so friendly that talking to you, we lost track of the journey!"

"See you guys tomorrow at 10 am," she zoomed off.

"What the fuck man! Are you people crazy? We are here to have fun together and you are calling that girl tomorrow, whom we know only for the last hour?" Surjeet thought we were crazy.

"So what's the problem dude? We will enjoy her company and she can call her other sweet, sexy friends over as well," Arvind said.

"Arvind is right! Please let her come tomorrow Surjeet," I said.

"Okay you womanizers," Surjeet said. "Let's go in."

Arvind jumped on the bed as soon we entered our room, screaming: "I want beer, beer, beer!"

"Catch dude," Surjeet threw a beer can towards Arvind. I also opened a beer and we started off drinking. Most of the people go on a trip to explore different places but what we were doing on the first day of our trip, was drinking!

By 7 pm we had downed almost 7 beers each. We were all in a good mood. Suddenly Arvind said, "Let's go to hell dude, and rock hell!!!" I got excited as London was all new to me but unlike Surjeet and Arvind I was looking forward to exploring London, parallel to drinking and partying.

"So where are we going?" I asked.

"Surprise!!" Surjeet said. In our intoxicated state we set out to enjoy London night life. We reached the club Surjeet chose, which he claimed was one of the best places to enjoy London's night life. Three of us entered the club and it was amazing and spectacular – with pounding trance music and plenty of Snow Whites, each better than the other.

We had a lot of fun there and then, on Arvind's recommendation, we went to a pole dance club.

"Nekman take out ten pounds, tip that hot waitress and watch the fun," Arvind said.

"Are you serious?"

"Come on Nekman, just do it man!"

"Okay, my brothers," I said. We all were drunk and had lost count of how many bottles of beer or pegs we had downed. It was a limitless night for us and we were on the verge of making Hangover Part 10.

"Hey Snow-White, please come here," I said.

I tipped the beautiful waitress ten pounds and what she did after that was epic! She made all her sexy moves, up, down, left, right and in front of me. She even sat on my lap which was irresistible as I was all wet - don't misunderstand; I was merely sweating from my exertions. It was just awesome! All three of us were surrounded by girls, unlike in India, where for every girl in a club there is a long queue of boys. In London, by God's grace, an abundance of girls seemed to exist and all of them - damn hot! For people of my age, it is heaven.

"See I told you, just ten pounds and the pleasure is yours," Arvind said.

"Nekman my boy, have one more peg," Surjeet urged.

"Enough. I am already drunk dude, can't take anymore," I said.

"Then you are not my brother," Surjeet said.

"Surjeet please don't behave like this; I am all done," I said.

"No, you are not my brother," Surjeet said again.

"Nekman, Nekman, Nekman…" Arvind sang, pouring a peg for me.

"No Arvind, I don't want it."

They began sing a jingle which all three of us had made up once:

"Drunkie Drunkie Drunkie Drunkie Drunkie...

1 peg 2 peg 3 peg if you are not a Drunkie then don't take another peg

Be a super moron who never wants self-respect

Be a super moron who never wants to win the game

Be a super moron who never wants to chase the dream

Be a super moron who never wants to be in gain

1 peg 2 peg 3 peg if you see yourself as moron then don't take another peg

If you are a Drunkie, then cheers with us and celebrate!!"

"Okay guys, I am a Drunkie and I will finish my peg to celebrate."

"You are my real brother," Surjeet said.

"Love you darling," I said.

"I love you too," Arvind said making dance moves towards Surjeet and me.

After we had got over our emotional intoxicated brotherhood bonding we jumped into the crowd with the beautiful Snow Whites and had great fun. Kisses and hugs were no big deal for girls present in the club, and loads of smooching and hugging happened that night. We ended our night with a song called 'Scream and Shout' by WILL.I.AM in the club.

7

Romeo-Juliet

Ting tong! Ting tong! Ting tong!

"Dude, what the fuck is this? Who is honking on our hotel room door, early morning?

"Shit man, stop it! Can't stand it! My head is pounding like hell," I said.

"Wait! I am going to the door, you lazy fellows," Surjeet said.

"Oh shit!" Surjeet suddenly smashed the door close again.

"What happened?" Arvind and I quavered.

"Rascals, your Silvana is outside," Surjeet said.

"Why so early?"

"Nekman bro its 11am and she must have been waiting the last hour," Arvind said.

"You people go ahead. I am tired, I am going to sleep," Surjeet mumbled.

"Come on dude, don't be a spoil sport, come with us."

"Brothers all this we can decide later, let her come in first she is standing outside the room," Arvind laughed.

"Oh yes, let me open the door," I leapt forward.

"Nekman!" Surjeet shouted but the warning came too late. I opened the door and realized I was wearing my red mermaid printed boxers and nothing else! It was the same with Arvind and Surjeet. But now I had to welcome her into the room as Surjeet had already slammed the door on her once.

"Hello Silvana, hey how are you? Come inside we were waiting for you," I said in a happy mode.

"What the hell? I've been waiting from 9:45 am, then I asked at Reception for your room and you people are still not ready!"

"No, it's not like that - we are almost ready. All we need is five minutes," Arvind said.

"Yes Silvana don't be angry - we just have to put on our clothes as we already showered last night to save time this morning," I said.

"Yes he is right and there is no need for clothes either, we will go in our boxers only as we planned that this would be our dress code for the day, right Nekman?" Surjeet said sarcastically.

"Guys, I will wait at the Reception. Please come down within 15 minutes and stop pulling each other's leg," Silvana said.

"Yes dear, we are coming," Arvind said blowing her a kiss which she didn't notice.

The moment she left, Arvind and I got ready at the speed of light to get to the Reception, while Surjeet showered leisurely.

"So Silvana where are you going to take us today? "Once again I had leapt for the front seat.

"First, let your friend come he is taking so much time."

"Oh, he will come down in a few minutes Silvana, but at least tell me where you will be taking the three of us," I said.

"London sightseeing, what else?"

"Okay," I didn't press her any further as she already seemed irritated and it had already turned 11:30 am, when we had asked her to come at 10 am sharp.

"Let's go," Surjeet opened the door of the cab.

So we started off without any intoxication, to see London. Clean roads, greenery everywhere, pleasant weather and last but not least, beautiful Snow Whites everywhere. We saw the Tower Bridge, London Eye, Westminster Abbey, Buckingham Palace and the Big Ben. Everything was so beautiful. I enjoyed it a lot more than Arvind and Surjeet, as they had lived there for two years for their post-graduation. The place was heavenly, probably that's why London is one of the costliest cities in the world.

After showing us the sights Silvana took us to a theater to watch a play. London has a long tradition of theatre, due to which the world greatest plays are performed here. When we entered the theater, only I was happy among the three of us, because I was the one who wanted to be an actor and loved this kind of entertainment. Arvind was a person with no love of creativity; he only loved money. Surjeet went along with it for the experience – While studying his MBA in London he hadn't attended a single theater performance or any cultural activity, as he had been busy exploring all the pubs and discos of London.

'I love you Romeo, I want to die in your arms," Arvind delivered Juliet's dialogue. The play was Romeo and Juliet and all were silently watching the performers with full concentration, till Arvind laughed out.

"What your friend is doing? Tell him to keep silent," Silvana hissed.

"Arvind, please be silent!" I said.

"Oops, sorry!" Arvind apologized to Silvana and all of us watched the play with full concentration.

Time passed. The play was almost over when suddenly my situation with Hinsa flashed into my mind - perhaps because the play was all about love and pain. I was upset all over again. We all rose from our seats the moment play was over.

"Ha ha, I love you, I love you Romeo," Arvind laughed.

"Ha ha, yes kiss me baby, kiss me one last time," Surjeet giggled.

"Hey guys come on! Enough fun you people have made of the play," Silvana said as she pulled up in front of our hotel.

"Silvana, even I love you," Arvind said in his intoxication.

"Don't worry, he is just kidding," Surjeet said in Arvind defense, as Arvind was very high that night almost nine pegs down.

"Relax, I know he is very high, no worries," Silvana said.

"Okay, bye Silvana," Surjeet said.

"Surjeet I will come in a while, after I take a walk," I said.

Silvana was about to leave but she noticed me that I didn't go up to my room, plus I had been silent from the time play got over. She parked her car in the parking lot and asked me if she could walk with me.

"Yes, sure," I said.

There was pin-drop silence everywhere. Silvana and I walked on for ten minutes.

"Hey, what happened? She finally asked.

"Nothing."

"Something happened I'm sure. I can see it in your eyes. You were disturbed seeing that play, if I am not wrong," she said.

"No, nothing like that."

"Girlfriend problems?"

I kept silent. She had understood that something had gone wrong with my relationship, but she was unaware about the bomb which had been dropped on me.

"You can tell me you know," she said softly.

"No, its fine," I was reluctant to open up because talking about my past would make me relive all the agony again.

"You don't have to discuss it if you're not comfortable with me," she said. "So tell me who all are in your family?"

I smiled a bit: "One younger brother, mom and dad. So who all are in your family?" I asked.

"No one."

"What?"

"Yes. My mom and dad were killed in a car accident when I was kid and I grew in an orphan home."

"Oh, I am sorry," I said.

"Don't be. Such is life. I don't complain. I respect God for what he has given me instead of hating Him for what I don't have," she said.

"But still, how you can be so happy? I mean why don't you complain to God?"

"You complain every day to God, am I right? Is anything is getting better?"

I listened in silence.

"I feel there is no use fighting with God because sometimes we are not able to realize that whatever happens is for our good. Why don't you think that maybe God had given you a little bad to save you from something really bad? So why complain to God when you have no idea of the future?"

"Yes, you are right," I said.

"Be happy Nekman. Life is short, so live each day to the fullest, then your past and future will automatically become good," she said.

Hmm, she was right. Another thing I took away from that conversation was 'never to complain about what God has not given or taken from you instead be thankful to God and respect all the things which God has given you, then your life will be something else.'

"Hey Silvana, thank you," I said.

"For what?"

"Nothing. Just your positivity."

"I am just thankful to God for whatever he has blessed me with. That's it. Also, I don't know the reason why you were so upset today, but please don't be upset anymore," she smiled.

I smiled back. "Silvana do you know a good place where we can go tomorrow?"

"What kind of good place do you want to go to?"

"A place where I can meet my inner self, where I can feel Life and the essence of nature."

She smiled at me and said, "Okay. Be ready at 5 am."

"What? It's 1 am right now, it's already so late."

"You want to meet your inner self?"

"Yes…"

"Then be ready I'll pick you up. Waking up your friends is your responsibility, if you want them to come along."

"Yes sure, I will be ready on time but I don't think they will come." I knew it would be next to impossible to rouse Surjeet and Arvind in another 3-4 hours.

She drove away with a wave and I ran to the room to take a power nap as in another 3-4 hours I had to get ready. Somewhere I was very confident that she would take me to a place I have never seen in my life before, and that I would feel better from the inside by imbibing its positive energies.

8

Being Human

It was 4:45am and I was standing on the road outside my hotel waiting for Silvana. The morning was quite fresh and I could feel the freshness in every breath. The wind was pure as the love of a mother, the clouds were clear as drop of water and the trees were green as if never kissed by the lips of the sun.

A car honked behind me. Yes, it was Silvana.

"Great, you are here before time today," Silvana smiled.

I climbed in beside her. "So where are we going?" I said.

"That's a surprise, be patient. What about your friends?"

"I didn't try to wake them up, because I knew it was next to impossible. I don't want to miss the beautiful experience which we are heading to, so let's leave quickly," I said.

She laughed at my eagerness and sensed that I wanted to be alone with her, which was true.

We reached a place 40 kms away from London. The roads were absolutely free of traffic, which helped us reach our destination within 45 minutes. I was disappointed. The place was not so beautiful, contradictory to what I had been dreaming of.

I was really surprised. I saw some pigs messing around in the mud and a bad smell hung in the air, similar to the smell of bagasse. A big ancient building was in front of me. It looked straight out of a Harry Potter novel. Finally Silvana took me inside that ancient building and on entering it I came to know it was a shelter for blind people.

"Silvana, where have you brought me?" I asked, confused.

"Wait. Just come and keep quiet," she said.

"But you told me we were going to a beautiful place," I protested. She placed her hand on my lips shutting me up and asked me to follow her.

We entered a big ball room where many blind people were housed. I watched them nervously; some of them were also dumb and deaf, but I was amazed to see the way they interacted with each other. Each was so efficient that they knew at what distance their belongings were kept and exactly how far the Reception was or the bathrooms were. I mean, they knew each and every corner of that building without ever having seeing it.

"Hey guys, I'm Silvana," she said loudly and clearly. All of them got a little curious but also smiled at the presence of Silvana. All were delighted, some of them started dancing and some shouted Silvana's name. They all celebrated the presence of Silvana and I was awestruck, wondering – "Am I with a superwoman?"

Silvana made me sit on a chair and calmed all of them down. "Hey everyone, I have a friend with me today, and he has come all the way from India to meet you. His name is Nekman, please say hi to him."

"Hi Nekman!" everyone shouted.

"Hi," I said to all.

Silvana told them that I had brought them a lot of surprise gifts from India. All were happy and I sat silently with a grin on my face, watching.

She asked all of them to shake hands with me and greet me. Everyone came forward, one by one, and shook my hand. I realized that they were far better organized and disciplined than people who can see the world with their eyes. After meeting them I became aware of why they were referred to as 'differently-abled', rather than as 'handicapped'.

Everyone shook hands with me and thanked me for the surprise gifts that I had brought them. They all interacted with me and gave me a feeling of being blessed, which was great.

There was nothing else on my mind all the time we were inside. We both came out and sat on a bench near the building. I was silent, mesmerized on seeing these people with different abilities who were kinder and more compassionate in comparison to us. After five minutes of silence I burst out crying. I cried a lot; I don't know why. Even Silvana's eyes filled with tears, at the way I was crying.

She didn't try to stop me. Just watched me sitting there with tears rolling down my face. I think she wanted me to let out all the negative energy and pain within me.

"Here, drink some water," she said finally.

I took a long sip.

"Are you okay? "

I nodded.

"Feeling better?"

I looked at her and said yes.

"Silvana, Can I tell you something?"

"Yeah, sure."

"Yesterday you asked me why I was so silent after watching Romeo-Juliet. The reason was - my engagement was called off recently, with a girl with whom I was in a serious relationship for the last three years. I gave my three years of my life to her and at one shot she went away from me."

"I am so sorry, but why did all of this happen?"

"It's a long story…maybe some other time," I said.

"Hmm, yes, leave it. Okay tell me, how are you feeling now?"

"Relaxed…like I've let out all the negative energy and pain."

"Good! Everything's poured out through your eyes and nose," she smiled.

"Yes," I smiled back.

"You found your inner self today and the happiness you were searching for?"

"To some extent."

I had been searching everywhere for peace and happiness, without finding it. That day, Silvana made me realize that the peace and happiness I was looking for was inside me, in my mind and in my heart, nowhere else.

I had always cribbed and complained about God for small reasons. I never acknowledged that God had given me so much - a beautiful family, friends, and most importantly, good health, which thousands of people don't have. So rather than complain, I should have been thankful to the Almighty. My visit to the Blind Center turned out to be a wonderful experience which I would have never had had if Silvana had not taken me there.

"Hey, what about the surprise gifts you promised all of them that I have brought?" I asked her.

She smiled, "Don't worry, I ordered the gifts before coming here and they have already been delivered at the Reception."

"Okay Superwoman, but tell me one thing, since when have you been coming here?"

"It's been long now... from when I was a teenager I started working and giving a bit of my salary to these places. My orphanage is also nearby. I visit it frequently to meet the smaller kids."

At that moment just one word came to mind: WOW! Silvana had a golden heart; she was far more beautiful on the inside than outside.

"Silvana, thank you."

"For what?"

"For the kind of experience you have filled me with."

She smiled: "It's just a bit of love which one can give to another and make oneself as well as others happy."

That day I imbibed some good things and promised myself to share the love in me with everyone.

"Hey, Arvind and I lied to you," I said.

"About what?"

Arvind and Surjeet are not new to London they have done their Master's degree here. We didn't tell you as we wanted your company. We were lucky to have such a beautiful, model-like chauffer," I smiled, looking at her.

"Are you serious? You are very bad! You made a fool of me!" She slapped my shoulder playfully.

"Surjeet was not a part of our plan. Sorry, don't take this the wrong way," I said.

"Relax, no problem. Even I enjoy being with the three of you. Let's go back now. If your friends wake up they may get upset with your absence – they don't even know where you are!"

"Upset? Not at all. They must be sleeping even now, it's only 8 am.'

"They are your best friends, right?"

"Yes and above all, they are not with me only in good times but stand with me in hard times too."

"You are lucky to have such good friends!"

"Yes I am lucky to have good friends – and now I believe one more name has been added to that list," I smiled.

"Who?"

"You."

"Seriously?"

"You are combination of outer as well as inner beauty," I said and paused.

She blushed a little and said mischievously: "Looks like someone is flirting around!"

"Please don't take it otherwise…"

"Cool - don't worry, just kidding. You are a very nice person."

"Really?"

"Yes!"

We both smiled and something passed between our eyes which was magical; I can't express it in words.

"Hey don't tell your friends that I'm from an orphanage. I don't want anyone to pity me."

"Sure. What do I tell them about where we've been? I don't want to tell them about the Blind Centre – they will laugh!"

"Tell them that we went to church."

"Hmm…" I nodded.

"Come, let's go back now. You are on holiday but I have work dude - and every day I can't abandon my job."

We got into the car and drove back.

Casino Night

It was our third day in London. We were heading to the casino. I told both Surjeet and Arvind that I had gone out with Silvana in the morning. Surjeet was fine with this as he hardly takes an interest in girls - he loves only his pegs and chicken; Arvind, on the other hand was quite jealous, and this put him in a bad mood.

"Come on let's leave," I said, as all of us were ready.

Surjeet and I went towards the door, but Arvind continued to lie in bed wearing his party clothes.

"Fucker Arvind, get up! Don't you want to go with us?" Surjeet shouted.

"No."

"Oh shit! Arvind don't tell me you are angry that I went to church with Silvana this morning!"

"Yes, I am angry - because we both decided to have fun with her," Arvind said.

"Give me a break bro - we went early morning and you were not in your senses last night which is why I didn't wake you up - and above all, she is not that kind of girl!"

"What do you mean she is not that kind of girl? We both planned to have fun with her and all girls here are game for one night stands."

"Yes I know, but she is not like that. When I spent time with her today, I realized it. Don't worry I have not 'enjoyed' with her as you imagine - we just went to church."

"I know you're lying, you must had ding dong with her!" Ding dong was our code for sex.

"I tell you Arvind, she is not like that, buddy; she's a good girl."

"Okay. So maybe you find her good because she gave you a good blow..." Before Arvind could say one more word I jumped on the bed and hit him.

A fight broke out between Arvind and me and suddenly, we heard the loud noise of splintering glass. All three of us turned around and saw that the television in our room had shattered.

"Oh fuck! You rascals, see what both of you have done!" Surjeet shouted.

Angry, Surjeet too jumped on the bed and began hitting both of us. We had all been well dressed for our casino night and now we were all in torn shirts.

"One day you guys will kill each other over girls," Surjeet muttered darkly.

Arvind and I look at each other and burst out laughing. Surjeet too joined in.

"But it was not my mistake, Arvind was wrong!"

"Okay dude, apologies," Arvind said.

"Let's all change our shirts and leave now, otherwise it will be too late for the casino," Surjeet said.

We left not knowing what to expect, but this is how that night turned out:

"Hey, look at that girl... wow! She's damn hot," Surjeet said. Arvind and I were amazed as Surjeet hardly goes for eye candy like we do; now, all of a sudden, he was frozen into position watching a girl.

"What? Where?"

"On the road opposite," Surjeet said.

"Wow! Damn hot man, I just love her," Arvind said.

"Yes she is amazing," I said. For about five minutes all three of us just stood there watching her, then we realized there was some problem with her car as she was searching for something.

"Come on, she needs our help. I think she has car trouble," Arvind said.

"Coming..." I said.

We ran across the road with Surjeet on our heels. Well it's true that girls can make any man go crazy - I was amazed to see Surjeet running for a girl - just a few minutes ago he had been lecturing Arvind and me against girls.

"Hey lady, do you need help?" I asked the beauty.

"No thank you."

"We are from London and we study in a university nearby, so can we help you," Arvind said.

"There is some problem with my car key, I don't know why the car door is not opening," she said.

"Oh please give me your key I will try to open the car." Arvind took the key, touching her pretty hands in the process.

Surjeet was just standing by, staring at her like he had never seen a girl before in his life.

"Dammit! It's not opening," Arvind stamped his foot.

"Let me try," I said.

Arvind threw the key at me.

I went to the car door with a confident smile to the beauty but, unfortunately, even I was not successful. We thought, perhaps, there was some problem with the key so we decided to call someone from a car workshop.

"Good idea – Nekman you go with Surjeet, I will stay here with this lady," Arvind said.

"No, I'll stay, you guys go," Surjeet said.

"Guys she is watching us," I whispered, "first let any one of us impress her then we can invite her to join us at the casino tonight."

"Okay - so I will impress her," Surjeet declared confidently.

"Great. Come Arvind, let's go," I said.

"No I want to be here," Arvind said.

"Please brother, let's go because Surjeet hardly demands anything on the girl front, let it go for now," I urged.

Arvind agreed. "Bye," Surjeet blew us a kiss jubilantly.

"So ma'am, are you from London?" Surjeet said.

"Yes," the white angel replied.

"What's your name?" Surjeet asked

Instead of answering, the beauty appeared to be struck by a thought and suddenly she ran towards the car boot, followed by a nonplussed Surjeet.

"Oh fuck! Shit! This is not my car," she exclaimed, looking at the number plate.

"What?? Then whose car is it?"

"I don't know and I am really sorry. Please ask your friends to come back!"

"Oh, not a problem, I will call them. Don't worry. Let me help you find your car," Surjeet said.

With love on his brain, Surjeet forgot everything, including me and Arvind, and walked off with her. Meanwhile, Arvind and I came back with a mechanic to get the door open.

"Hey, what the hell? Where is Surjeet and the chick?" Arvind said.

We looked around the car and they were nowhere to be found.

"Okay leave it, they must be around here somewhere. Let's get this door open and call Surjeet's phone once it's done."

"Okay, but I am not going to call him, he must have gone for ding dong," Arvind laughed.

"Come on dude, in five minutes no girl is going to be ready for ding dong and especially with Surjeet," I said and both of us laughed.

Five minutes later, the car door was opened and the mechanic left. Arvind and I got into the car and waited for Surjeet and the hot chick to show up. Suddenly two extra-large, six-footers came and banged on the car door. Startled, we jumped out.

"What the hell do you think you are doing?" I shouted.

"Kid, shut your mouth! I should be asking you that. What the hell you are doing in our car?" one of the hulks demanded in a tone bristling with aggression.

"What?? Hey dude, give me a break - this is our car, you understand? Just fuck off," Arvind said.

I don't know how Arvind dared to ask them to fuck off seeing the hulking sizes of their bodies and knowing what they were capable of doing. The result was that the hulk took hold of Arvind by his collar.

"Let go of him, you fuckers!" I jumped into the fray and found myself in the firm grasp of the other hulk.

Suddenly, I spotted Surjeet strolling along, lost in his own world.

"Surjeet!" Arvind and I shouted.

"Hey dudes, what are you people up to?" Surjeet asked, surprised.

"What do you think? We are being banged up by these hulks who are saying that this car belongs to them," I said.

"Where is the girl?" Arvind asked Surjeet.

"Oh fuck! I forgot to call you people," Surjeet said.

"First please call the girl, so she can tell these hulks that she is the owner of this car."

"But these gentlemen are right, this car belongs to them. Actually that chick got confused as she is has the same model, but the moment she saw the number plate, she ran towards her own car - I went with her and I forgot to tell you people to come back."

"What the fuck??" Arvind and I shouted at Surjeet.

"Kids, now let's go for a ride," one of the hulks said, before we could make our apologies.

They threw the three of us into the back of the car and sped towards a lonely road. All three of us shouted like kids till they showed us a beautiful Smith & Wesson revolver, after that we maintained pin-drop silence. Fifteen minutes went by and we reached a crowded street of London, unfamiliar to Surjeet and Arvind. The street was bathed in florescent colors - red, pink, green, blue, etc. The street seemed to be a miniature of Las Vegas, with crowded pubs. There was something seedy about the place. All three of us sensed that something bad was going to happen. The hulks ordered us to follow them and on seeing the revolver in their hands, we followed them quietly.

"We are finished!" Arvind whispered to both of us.

"Yes, we are going to get fucked tonight," I said.

"It's your mistake, you fucker!" Arvind hissed at Surjeet.

"Why? What did I do? I just forgot to make one call, that's it," Surjeet said.

"Forgot to call? Dammit, we opened someone else's car and told them to fuck off. We're all going to be killed soon because of you!"

"Okay, fine! What do you want? I suggest, first both of you kill me, and then get yourselves killed by the hulks!"

"Silence!" the hulk shouted, "We are entering the Banana Babuna Club."

"Banana Babuna? Who's that?" Arvind asked.

"He is our boss - head of the underworld mafia and owner of this club," the other hulk said.

Slack-jawed, the three of us entered the club which was full of bananas - the lamp was banana-shaped, the chairs were banana-shaped, even the wallpaper was printed with bananas! The hulks took us to the top floor, to the room where Banana Babuna sat.

"Boss," one of the hulks said to Banana Babuna who was sitting at a big table with four to five dozen bananas it. Mr. Babuna was eating one of the bananas himself. The room looked like a banana warehouse, rather than a mafia den.

"These kids were trying to steal our car."

"No we were not," I said.

"Actually there was some confusion sir, that's why this all crap happened," Surjeet tried to explain.

"Yes, we are not liars, sir," Arvind chimed in.

"Sit, handsome Indians," a heavy voice came from the table. Yes, it was Mr. Banana Babuna himself, ordering the three of us to sit in front of him. We sat, chanting God's name under our breath, believing that at any moment a trigger would be pulled from a gun pointing at us.

"Do you people know how important that car is to me?" Mr. Babuna asked.

"Very important sir, it seems to be an expensive car," Arvind said.

"No, it's not the price of the car," Mr. Babuna said.

"Then what, sir?" I asked.

"In the boot of that car there are fifteen dozen Australian bananas and these were sent from Australia by my first wife and I think you people must be in a plot to steal my bananas, right?

All three of us goggled at Mr. Babuna wondering if he was actually a comedian. We were secretly amused to see a human being so mad about bananas. In my mind, I thought Mr. Babuna must have been a monkey in his previous birth.

"No sir, nothing like that. We didn't even know there were bananas in the boot," Arvind tried to defend us.

"Don't lie. Just stay quiet, you three!" One of the hulks ordered.

Mr. Babuna threw a box of playing cards towards me and asked me to distribute them among the four of us. Arvind, Surjeet and I looked at each other and wondered how, instead of a casino party, we had landed up in a dingy place playing cards with Mr. Banana Babuna. What a fucking, crazy night!

I dealt the cards with jittery hands. The biggest surprise came when Mr. Babuna revealed the rules of the game:

"There are two rules to this game," he said. "First, if you three lose you have to be my servants for life."

"But sir..."

"Be quiet, I'm not done yet," Mr. Babuna continued, "the second rule of the game is that if you people win, you have to die!"

"All three of us felt half-dead just listening to this. Seeing which, all the goons surrounding us, including Mr. Babuna, burst out laughing.

"Sir, please let us go, we had no intentions of stealing your bananas," Surjeet pleaded.

"Start the game," Mr. Babuna shouted.

Five minutes passed. We were playing poker and no one was good at it, except Arvind, and that too only at online poker, but it was good that none of us were any good, because if we won, according to Mr. Babuna's rules, we would be killed. Only if we lost, by default our breath could continue.

At the end of the game everyone displayed their cards and we lost. At least we knew we weren't going to die, but on other hand, to be servant of Mr. Babuna was not a good deal as we would die every day working with the hulks.

Everyone laughed at when we lost the game. We were in a hellish situation and it all felt hopeless till my eyes fell on a photograph on the wall behind Mr. Babuna – it was a picture of Silvana's orphanage! The picture appeared to be at least a decade old. In it Mr. Babuna was standing with two little girls. Like a divine light an idea entered my head which could save all three of us from Mr. Babuna's spider web.

10

Casino Night-Unplugged

"Mr. Babuna from now on we are your servants and we will have no time for friends. So can we say goodbye to our dear friend whom we have come to meet London?" I said.

Arvind and Surjeet looked at me astonished, wondering what I was up to. I signaled to them to keep silent and go along.

"Okay, you can call your friend but keep it short." Mr. Babuna was feeling generous.

I began to call Silvana from my mobile phone.

"What the fuck? Why are you calling her?" Arvind was watching me closely

"Just wait and see."

"Hello, Silvana? Can you come to meet us right now?" I spoke at bullet speed.

"Hey, calm down. What happened?

"Nothing happened, just please come."

"Relax dude and tell me what happened."

"Silvana I can't tell you, just please come," I said desperately

"Fine. Tell me where."

I gave her directions and urged her to make haste. I was hoping against hope that she and Mr. Babuna might have shared some orphanage connection which would make him view our case sympathetically.

One and a half hours went by and we were still waiting for Silvana to arrive. Meanwhile the three of us had been assigned chores and we got to work. The thought of peeing bananas all our lives was disgusting!

Suddenly we heard a female voice from outside Mr. Babuna's room. I assumed it must be Silvana and I was right. Silvana had arrived and was being scanned by a security guard.

She entered the room and saw the three of us and then Mr. Babuna. After a fraction of second, she moved toward Mr. Babuna and whispered in his ear for a good ten minutes.

"You people can leave," Mr. Babuna said indicating the three of us.

We were stunned and relieved and wondered what Silvana had said to him to get him to release us instantly.

"Thank you baby," Silvana said to Mr. Babuna.

"Bye sweetheart, take care and thank you."

The hulks tagged along us to see us off. As soon as we emerged from Mr. Babuna's trap, we shouted and screamed like anything.

"Thank you Silvana, so much," Surjeet said.

"You are a magician Silvana," Arvind said. "But what did you whisper in Mr. Babuna's ear that without a second thought, he released us?"

"Yes Silvana, what did you tell him?" Surjeet said.

"I told him that you people had AIDS and you could infect the bananas."

"What? Seriously you said this?" Arvind said.

Silvana had neatly side-stepped giving Arvind and Surjeet the orphanage story.

We laughed till our sides hurt and thanked Silvana again for her brilliant rescue. That time even Surjeet and Arvind's attitudes towards Silvana changed and they believed me when I said that she really was a girl with a rare kind of humanity.

"But how did you guys get into this trap?" Silvana said.

"Long story, cannot tell you right now," I said.

"So, what next?" Silvana said.

"We planned a casino night but unfortunately ended up playing cards with Mr. Babuna!" Surjeet said.

"Yes. Now no more plans after this bullshit," Arvind said.

All three of us were low on energy and ready to head to our hotel.

"Hey, you guys want to go for a nice jungle camp party with lots of booze and girls?" Silvana asked. We were already drooling in anticipation.

"Yes! Sure!" We couldn't agree fast enough.

Silvana laughed and drove us to the party. That's how our casino night ended. Looking back, it was quite an adventure, like a proper movie sequence starring, Mr. Banana Babuna and the Dirty Hulks.

Every night at London was full of activity, lights, colors, girls, booze and so on. We celebrated every night of our London trip. It would have been wonderful if I would have spent my rest of the life in the same manner, but a quite different reality awaited away from this dream world.

I had left all my worries and all my pain far behind when I was in London and was afraid that they would return to haunt me, but I had no other option but to go back to India.

Goodbye London.

11

Flash Black

"I never thought that someone like you would come into my life," Hinsa said.

I was lying in her lap and she was adoring me - her hands stroking my forehead and kissing me every minute. We were in a hanging garden nearby, where we use to sit for hours for the price of an entry ticket costing Rs.10 per person; it was the most pocket friendly and peaceful place for us at that time as we both were students. I was in my first year of MBA. In first year there is no placement pressure and lectures are also fewer compared to the second year, so I usually got to spend a lot of time with Hinsa. She was doing an interior designing course which did not demand the laborious study of an MBA.

"Do you mean that?" I asked her

"Yes baby, you are my life. Even my family hasn't given me the kind of love that you have given. You're the only one in this world for me," she said.

"Love you baby, always be with me. Never leave me alone, ever." I murmured.

"Yes my baby I will always be, but…"

"But?"

"At one point I might have to leave you."

"What are you saying?"

"When I will die I have to leave this universe and even you."

"Shut up! Don't talk like this Hinsa, we will always be together," I said with a sentimental tear and kissed her.

"Stupid, don't worry even if I die, I will come back as an angel in your life."

"Please stop. I don't care for this kind of negative talk." I was a little annoyed.

"Okay, sorry baby, no more of this I promise," she kissed me again, this time on my lips, creating that moment of silence when angels drift by.

As a person, I was very emotional inside. But, yes, one thing I have to admit was that I showed my emotional side only to girls. As for friends and family, I hardly paid any attention to them – especially once I had fallen in love. I realized later that I had literally ignored my family and friends during this period.

"Hinsa?"

"Yes baby?"

"You know I am doing an MBA - but I must tell you frankly that I'm still confused about what I want to do in life."

"Why? What does my baby want to do?"

"I really don't know, Hinsa."

"Okay listen, you know the person who helped me to shape my career and point the way to interior design was you. There was no support from my family but you gave me confidence and encouraged me to pursue the career I wanted."

"Yes I know, but things are different in my case - I have already paid fees for my MBA and now I have to do a 9-6 job after completing the course."

"Nekman, don't think like that."

"Then what should I think? You know what I have always wanted in life and now see where I have landed."

"Baby, I know your dream is to become an actor."

"Yes exactly - so why I am doing an MBA I really don't know."

"Please don't get upset, education always pays off Nekman and you are doing this MBA for me."

"For you?"

"You are upset that for no reason you are doing an MBA, so just think you are doing it for me. See, after two years both of us will be of marriageable age. By that time my baby should be earning enough to marry me."

"Hmm…" I agreed.

"Once we are married I will give you my full support baby. We'll move to Mumbai. I will work till you crack an audition and once my baby gets enough work, I will enjoy myself day and night on my husband's earnings."

Just hearing the word 'husband' got me emotional and I hugged her tight for showing me so much support and love. I never imagined that these promises which we made to each other would vanish into nothingness someday.

Ting tong, ting tong! The doorbell rang, interrupting my flashback. An hour ago I had turned on some porn on my laptop and got into this flashback of my ex-love story. I had returned from London, that morning, to an empty house - dad was away on an official trip, Joy was at an IIT entrance class and mom had gone to the temple.

Ting tong, ting tong! The doorbell rang again. It must be mom. I ran to the door, switching my laptop to sleep mode.

"Hi mom!" I shouted as I opened the door.

"My son!" Mom hugged me tightly. "How was your trip Nekman?"

"I will tell you everything but first come and see. I have brought a lot of surprises for you, Joy and dad - let me show you that first," I said.

"Okay. But let's wait for Joy. He will be back anytime now. He missed you very badly."

"I missed him too. Alright, let's wait for him."

"So now tell me how your trip was," she asked again.

"Awesome mom, I enjoyed myself - it is an awesome country. London is like a dream land, everything is just amazing over there whether it's people, cars, roads, music or the lifestyle of the people there - everything is just out of the world."

"Good. I'm happy my son enjoyed it so much," she kissed me on my forehead. "Today I have prepared very special food for my bulldog." She affectionately calls me her bulldog.

"Hello big brother!" Joy shouted the moment he entered home.

I hugged him tightly.

"Hey, how are you champ?" I asked.

"Good bro, how are you and how was London?"

"Awesome!"

"And what you have got for me?"

"Nothing."

His face fell.

"Mom, big bro is very bad - he didn't bring me anything. I had especially asked for an Apple iPod," he complained and assaulted me with a cushion.

"Stop that, Joy!" mom said in a laughing tone. "Your big brother has brought lots of surprises for you - he is just pulling your leg!"

"Really?"

"Yes, my potato," I replied.

"Mom he is calling me 'potato'," Joy attacked me with the cushion again.

"Nekman don't make fun of him."

"Okay, sorry," I laughed.

My mom was very happy seeing me laugh after a long time. I could see the relief in her eyes. Before I left I had been depressed and emotionally fragile but after my engagement but hanging out in London with my best buddies had been the best tonic ever.

"Come Joy let me show you the surprise I have got for you, which also includes your Apple iPod. "The moment I uttered iPod he jumped up and rushed into my room.

I felt very happy seeing my brother and mom enjoying the gifts I had bought. Even dad would have been happy but unfortunately he was on a job tour. After the gifts were handed over, mom, Joy and I sat down to the delicious lunch that mom had prepared. My mom was the best cook in this world for me and after so many days I was eating home food which made it made doubly delicious. The long menu included vegetable grilled sandwiches, pizza, roast chicken with salad, brownies with hot chocolate fudge and my favorite, hazelnut cold coffee. My mom was a master chef who could prepare dishes of any country.

12

Achievers – I

Two days after coming back from London, so as to not forget the purpose behind the London trip, which was to achieve our goals, work hard and make something of our lives, I created a group on WhatsApp called Achievers. The idea of creating a common group was to remind us every day, whenever we chatted, that we had to achieve what we dreamed of.

"Achievers? What the fuck is this?" Arvind texted back immediately.

"Dude, don't forget the reason why we went to London," I replied.

"What reason?" Surjeet jumped in.

"That we work hard and achieve something in life."

"Right Nekman. Let's gear ourselves up," Surjeet wrote.

"Let's start our day with positive energy and try to do our best," I texted.

"Cheers!!" This was Surjeet's favorite jargon.

It was Monday morning – time to make a new beginning at work with a lot of positive energy. I finished my glass of buttermilk and left for office without taking my lunch or eating breakfast.

"Son at least take your lunch - it will be ready in five minutes," mom shouted as I rushed out.

"No mom, got to rush or I'll get late to work," I shouted back, jumping into my car.

9 am and I was in my cubicle before my boss arrived. I was fully motivated now to do something in life, leaving my past behind. I promised myself not to indulge in flashblacks anymore (I say flash black instead of flashback as all was dark in my recollections).

"Nekman, good morning," Suraj said as he passed my cubicle.

"Hi Suraj - very good morning," I replied.

"Come to my cabin I need to talk to you."

"Coming boss."

"So, how was your trip to London?" Suraj said.

"It was awesome sir."

"Great - that means you had fun with a lot of butterflies over there."

"No sir," I laughed.

"Good. So Nekman, as I've already told you, your honeymoon period is over, so now get serious and get on to the clients as soon as possible."

"Yes sir."

"I need two things from you," he said. "First, you have to make a document regarding the business proposition of network as a practice, including all the technologies which we offer in our portfolio and second, a presentation on any one technology under the network, which you think you can master and can pitch to clients."

I simply nodded - as this just bounced off me without making a dent in my understanding.

"Yes sir, I will do it," I mumbled. I had the bad habit of saying yes to everything even when I wasn't sure if I could complete the task or not.

"Good - and I want you to present this on the presentation deck on the last day of the week, this Friday, because I want you to start pitching it to clients from next week. Any doubts?" Suraj asked.

"No sir," I said and returned to my seat without a word. Nothing of what Suraj said had registered with me. It was as if he had been speaking an alien language.

I was very nervous about the presentation. I hadn't attended the training sessions with any seriousness as I had been obsessing over my break up.

I started surfing the internet for information. Two hours later I was still blank. Even the all-knowing Google which has the answer to every damn thing was of no help with my presentation document. It was not Google's fault. Being from a non IT or engineering background I found it difficult to understand the terminologies of the IT industry and its framework. Pissed off, I just shut down my laptop.

"Hey, what happened Nekman?" Sonupriya asked me. She was in same team in which I was and had given me the chocolates which I mentioned before.

"Nothing.

I am just pissed off. I am trying so hard to understand the technologies but nothing is going into my head," I said.

"Oh, I can understand that. Being a guy from a non-techie background it must be difficult for you to grasp the technologies," she said

"Yes, right, but what to do now? I am all blank and this morning Suraj gave me two tasks – I don't know what to do."

"Hey don't get frustrated, I know it will take time but nothing is impossible and believe me IT is no rocket science.

You just have to read up on the basics of technology, there is no need to study in-depth the architecture of technologies."

"Yes I know, but I am not able to do even that."

"Nekman do you drink alcohol?"

"Yes," I said, slightly annoyed that she was switching to a discussion on alcohol while I was still worrying about the presentation,

"So if you drink a full bottle at one go what will happen?"

"I will vomit."

"Exactly! You are trying to learn everything in one single day that is your problem, and it will lead you nowhere. Bifurcate your work and learn technologies breaking it into small chapters every day, then automatically things will get easy."

"Yes, you are right," I said.

"Don't worry I am there for you, whenever you need help just come to my desk."

"Yes sure, thank you."

"No 'thank you's' between you and me - just get me a chocolate instead," she smiled.

"Sure," I smiled back.

This was the reason why she was the only one with whom I shared my pain over Hinsa. She used to take the weight off my mind every time I discussed any problem with her. She was clear-headed and always clam and composed.

So after talking to her, I divided my task so that I could achieve it step by step without further panic attacks.

At 8:45 pm I was still at work. As it was the first day of Achievers, I was highly motivated. Sometimes working late hours in the office gives you a motivational high. That day I kept working till 10 pm before I left for home. On the way back, I called Arvind.

"Hey brother, how are you?" I asked.

"All good man, how was your day in office?"

"It was good - pretty hectic. Just trying to catch up with all the learning which I didn't do in the training period. Hey, have you researched a business plan for yourself?" I asked.

"No not yet. Today I was busy the whole day as I went to a temple out of Delhi. I'll do it tomorrow."

"Arvind, don't take it lightly brother. We have to achieve something in our lives, remember? That's why I've named our group 'Achievers'.

"Yes Nekman, I will remember. Hey wait for a second Surjeet is calling, I will put him on conference."

"Hey brothers, how are you guys?" Surjeet said.

"All good. So Surjeet have you decided anything about your business?" I asked.

"Yes bro," Surjeet said. "I'm planning to open a mobile showroom."

"Great news," I said.

"Surjeet, don't tell me you are going to sell mobile phones for a 200-300 rupee margin after running a construction business where you had a margin of lakhs!" Arvind laughed.

After completing his studies in London, Arvind became a stereotype – one of those who would only go for a big business setup, nothing small.

"No Arvind, don't talk like this. At least he is trying something, we should motivate him," I said.

"Nekman, thank you my brother, and Arvind, the day will come when I will open a chain of mobile stores - you just wait and watch!" Surjeet said.

"Hey Surjeet, don't get angry, I was kidding bro. It's your choice. Don't take my words seriously," Arvind said.

"Cool. I am about to reach home, I will talk later." All three of us hung up.

I parked my car in the building parking lot and sat for five minutes. I prayed that each and every day would be as productive as this one and would make me more hard working. I also prayed that God would not give me any more setbacks now, after the difficulties with Hinsa. Deep down I knew I would have to face a big hurdle in the coming days, getting over that would be my biggest challenge: it was the day when Hinsa would marry someone else. I knew that sooner or later this would happen and I didn't know how I was going to survive that. I just prayed that when the time came, God would give me strength.

13

Achievers – II

When you are fully immersed in work, you don't even realize how fast time passes by and soon you have a weekend at your doorstep. Yes, it was Friday. I had been working day and night for my word document and presentation which I had to present to Suraj. The whole week had whizzed past at the speed of light. I had read a lot and worked hard, to the best of my ability, to show my manager that I could be an agent of change for the organization.

"Hi Nekman!" Sonupriya came to my desk. "So finally it's the day of your presentation to Suraj."

"Yes, but I am a little nervous. I don't know what to expect at that meeting."

"Don't worry, whatever you have prepared just present it with full confidence."

"Nekman, block the meeting room for two hours, I will take your presentation. Sonupriya, you also come along," Suraj ordered.

"Oh fish! Now what should I do?" I was already feeling hassled.

"Chill, be confident, you will perform well and now I will be there to support you."

It's easy to say 'be confident', I thought sourly, but when your mind is in a jumble your confidence evaporates!

I blocked a meeting room as instructed by Suraj, and waited there with Sonupriya. The best thing about our meeting rooms were the free chips and biscuits and the first thing Sonupriya and I did was order them from the pantry.

Five minutes went by, waiting for Suraj to arrive. The pantry boy came in with the chips, biscuits and coffee. I had just started on the chips when Suraj came into the meeting room.

"Hello sir," I said mouth half full.

"Hello! Are you enjoying yourselves?" Suraj asked jovially and snagged two biscuits for himself. Suraj was a chilled out boss in general, but when it came to work he was damn strict, which was reasonable in a boss.

"Nekman, let's start with the presentation. You can mail the word document to me. I will see it later on."

"Okay sir," I said.

"Go ahead. Start your presentation."

I took a deep breath, chanted God's name in my mind and stood up to begin my presentation. 15 minutes passed and I was still talking. Even I didn't know what I was speaking, but somehow at the end of 15 minutes my confidence got a boost. Suraj hadn't interrupted me even once. I began to feel sure that this time I would get a pat on my back. Being an imaginative person, it doesn't take much to send me dreaming.

"Any questions?" I looked at Sonupriya and Suraj.

Sonupriya just said 'good' and didn't ask any questions, even if she had any queries she would not have voiced them as her intention was to support me.

"I have few questions," Suraj said.

"Yes sir, ask away," I said with a grand filmy gesture, as if I knew the answer to every damn question.

The illusion was quickly shattered when Suraj asked me list of questions and I was not able to answer a single one!

"Nekman, it was a fair attempt by you. You have put in a lot of effort in the presentation but you still have a long way to go." Suraj said.

"Yes, sir. I will definitely try to improve."

"Good! I appreciate your effort and your confidence. Keep it up and take it to the next level," Suraj said

"Thank you sir!" I was elated. At least he had appreciated my efforts and boasted my morale - that was enough for me because my morale was very low those days, but at that moment I gained back some of my confidence.

"Hey champ, you did well," Sonupriya said.

"Thank you for your help, without that I would have not able to present this much even," I said.

"No Nekman, it's all your dedication towards work, which you have shown."

I was gaining my confidence back, I was working hard according to the Achievers plan, yet, somewhere in my heart and mind I knew I was not in the right job. After my presentation with Suraj, I seriously considered whether I was heading in the right direction. I had always dreamt of becoming an actor, a famous personality of Bollywood, but now I was doing nothing to achieve that dream.

The big question in my mind was: would working towards that unpredictable goal make me an achiever someday? I didn't have an answer.

"Hey Nekman, where are you lost? Come, let's go for lunch," Sonupriya said.

"You go. I have some work. I will have lunch after." I was still puzzling over my choice of career.

After she left I continued to sit in the meeting room, deep in thought.

At 8:30 pm I left office and called Arvind. He said he had been trying Surjeet all day. We tried his line once more and put him on conference.

""Surjeet where are you brother? You didn't take Arvind's or my calls," I said.

"So sorry guys, I was about to call you – actually, I finalized land for my mobile store today. So I was busy with legal documents," Surjeet said.

"What?? Are you seriously opening a mobile store?" Arvind sounded shocked

"Great news Surjeet, congratulations!" I said quickly.

"Congratulation dude! That's a bull's eye, great going!" Arvind followed my lead.

"Thank you, both of you - now just pray it opens soon and makes a lot of profit!" Surjeet said.

"Sure brother, we will pray for you," Arvind and I said.

"So guys, where's the party tonight?" I asked.

"Anywhere. Today is Surjeet's day, wherever he suggests, we will go," Arvind said.

"Sorry brothers, no drinks for me for the next forty days," Surjeet said. Arvind and I were shocked that Surjeet would even contemplate not drinking.

"Why? What happened?"

"Nothing – it's just that I have undertaken a forty day fast in which I am not going to drink alcohol or eat non-veg," Surjeet said.

Arvind laughed: "This is all for the new store Nekman!"

"Yes Arvind," I also laughed at Surjeet - but it was a good step as it showed that Surjeet was serious about implementing his goals, like we had decided.

Surjeet was the first one to initiate something as per Achievers, whereas Arvind had still not fixed on an idea and neither was he making any effort to do so. As for me, I was doing well in my job, but still struggling with the question of whether this was what I wanted to do all my life.

———∿∿———

14

Good Times

"Congratulations brother!" Arvind and I shouted, entering Surjeet's brand new mobile store.

Yes Surjeet had finally opened his mobile store after a lot of hard work and we were obviously on the top of the list of invitees to his store opening. A bunch of Sikh uncles were present there, with big moustaches and beards and with colorful turbans on their heads. The most amazing part of Surjeet's mobile store opening was, that instead of cold drinks Surjeet's dad had arranged for chilled beer at 10 am in the morning. As I mentioned earlier Surjeet's dad was in love with hard drinks. "Thank you so much brothers," he replied.

"Hey, we got something for you," Arvind said.

"What?"

"It's a surprise. Open it and see," I said. We rarely bought gifts for each other, but, as it was a special day in Surjeet's life, Arvind and I had made the effort.

"Okay, let me open it," Surjeet said. The moment he opened the parcel he became very happy. Surjeet's mom came forward to see what we got.

"It's beautiful. Jai Guru Nanak ji," Surjeet mom said. We had got him a big, framed, Guru Nanak Dev photograph. Guru Nanak Dev is one of the patron saints of the Sikhs.

"Thank you brothers," Surjeet. In between this sequence Surjeet's dad came, looked at the photograph and bowed his head. After that he turned and shouted to Arvind and me: "What the hell are you people doing inside the store?"

"What happened uncle?" Arvind asked

"Come on, young guns I have arranged chilled beer outside, go and take your glass," Surjeet's dad said.

"Thank you uncle, but it's too early for a drink," I said.

"What?? Be a man! Go and grab a beer and I don't want to listen to excuses. Now go and enjoy!"

"Oh God, why are you are forcing these kids to drink alcohol?" Surjeet's mom came into the picture.

"My sweet wife, come on, they are no longer kids. Let them enjoy. Hey, go fast," Surjeet dad shooed us out and we ran toward the bar with a smile on our faces. Just for formality's sake we had pretended that we didn't want to drink, but secretly we were in full mood for chilled beer."

"Cheers! The beer is damn chill," I said as all three of us took our first sip.

"Hey Surjeet, why aren't you drinking your beer? Your forty days are over now," Arvind said.

"Because my family is here I am drinking slowly dude," Surjeet said.

"Hey Nekman, why so serious?" Arvind asked.

"I was just thinking... actually there's something I want to share with both of you."

"What?"

"I have a surprise for my mom and dad," I said.

"Great! What surprise dude?"

"You guys have to come with me; I will not disclose the surprise. The delivery time of the surprise is around 2 pm so you people just come along with me and I will show it to you there itself," I said.

"Sorry but I can't came along with you Nekman. I have to take care of guests - today is the opening day," Surjeet said.

"Yes I know, you attend to your guests and come over to my place this evening. I too will reach home by evening only," I said.

"Arvind can go with you," Surjeet said.

"Yes buddy, let's go, even I am eager to see what surprise you are planning for your mom and dad," Arvind said.

At 8 pm that night, I got home with a small box wrapped up nicely in a florescent colored wrapper. Arvind and Surjeet joined me outside the house. They both knew what the surprise was.

"Mom, open the door!" I shouted in excitement. Though there was a doorbell, my excitement made me shout.

"Coming son," she replied from kitchen.

"Hey mom, where is dad?" I asked.

"Your dad is in bedroom. What happened?" mom asked.

"Call him I have got a surprise for both of you." I said.

"Son, what are you doing?"

"Nothing - just call dad fast mom," I said and called Joy too, to come to the dining room.

"Hi big brother!"

"Hey, I've got a surprise for mom and dad," I said to the three of them in the dining room.

"What is it Nekman?" dad asked.

I stood quietly for a minute just looking at mom and dad, then slowly took out the beautifully wrapped box from my pocket and presented it to them.

"Nekman what is this?"

"Just open it."

"You open it," mom told dad.

They opened the box and in it was a key.

"What is this son?" dad asked.

"Both of you came outside and I will show you." Well, by now, they may have guessed what waited for them, but they couldn't believe it.

We came outside. Surjeet and Arvind were already waiting with my 'surprise' - a brand new hatchback car with an average of 17 kmpl. Yes, this was my surprise, especially for dad. I didn't want him to travel by Metro at the age of 56. There was silence for a minute, then mom was in tears and my dad hugged me tightly and kissed me. Joy was also very excited and he ran to the car and got in.

"Son, what is this? Why are you spending your savings like this?" dad asked.

"Installments, dad. No need to worry, only a small down payment. From now on, you are going to office in this car – no ifs and buts," I said.

"No son…" dad demurred.

"Dad, I especially chose a car with good mileage and you are still protesting?"

"Your son has given it with so much of love and affection, now you must use it regularly," mom said.

"Okay," dad hugged me again.

This surprise was mainly for dad but I did not forget the person who was everything to me in the universe, my guide, my philosopher, my mom.

"Mom, there is one more surprise."

"Now what?"

I took a second box from my pocket and handed it to my mom.

"This is for you."

She just opened and exclaimed: "Wow!!" In it was a brand new Apple iPhone 4S which was the Godfather of all available phones at that time. She hugged me and kissed me with tears in her eyes.

"Come on, enough of emotional drama - let's go for a ride in our new car," I said.

"Yes my son. Call Arvind, Surjeet inside. Let them have some sweets, then we can all go for a ride." Sweets are the most important part of any Indian celebration.

At 1 am I was lying in bed with tears in my eyes, tears of happiness. This was the first time in my life that the tears rolling down my face were of happiness. I had made my mom and dad proud of me, although that pride was going to cost me a five thousand rupee deduction from my salary every month. Fifty percent of my savings were already gone towards down payment for the car. Yet, that was just a small price to pay for my mom's and dad's smiles.

One thing I must say, people say money can't buy happiness, its true, but it can buy at least temporary happiness. One should not run after money day and night, but must earn enough to satisfy a basic need or basic luxury, what every individual wants in this modern world.

All in all, that was one of the most memorable days of my life. Yet that night, like every other, I was haunted by two questions: the first involved Hinsa. Was she a part of my destiny? Even though my engagement had been called off I still had hopes that some miracle would happen and we would be together again. Yes I knew - miracles happened only in fairytales yet, I could not let go of the dream.

The second big question was, where was I going with my career? But, at least I was going to take some steps to resolve this question.

I planned to join a theater group in Delhi. This would allow me to test out my capabilities and know, once and for all, whether my childhood dream of being an actor was a possibility that I should seriously pursue.

Lights! Camera! Nekman!

Good night.

———∽∽∽———

15

Lights! Camera! Nekman! – I

That night I researched many theater groups around Delhi and the best one I came across was a theater group that rehearsed only on weekends.

The theater group's selection criteria was that members must work in the corporate sector and undergo an audition. It was one of the few good things that happened to me in those bad times. I had found a theater group that suited my office schedule. I cleared the audition and made it to my first rehearsal which was scheduled on a Friday night at 8 pm.

It was raining heavily that night. I was lucky enough to have a car thanks to which I reached my rehearsal on time, without a problem. The moment I entered the rehearsal hall I saw that it was crowded with 18-20 people standing around. I was immediately nervous, as, for the past one year I hadn't participated in any stage performance, caught up as I had been in finding a job and then with my relationship.

"Hi Namrata," I said. She was the director who had approved my audition. In addition to doing theatre she also ran a placement agency.

"Nekman?" she had not taken my audition earlier, as if she had never seen me before, and after asking my name went back to her book.

She seemed absorbed with whatever she was reading and the rest of the people too, were busy with some or the other task, some talking within themselves, some reading, some busy with writing and no one even bothered to glance towards me. They seemed unaware that a new candidate had arrived. It was a little nerve-wracking. I had heard that theater artists are always in their own world, and that day, watching them, I believed it was true.

"Namrata?" I said.

"Yes?" she said without taking her eyes from her book.

"I just wanted to know that what I'm supposed to do in rehearsal," I said.

"For today, just read any of the books kept in the rack near the entrance door." Her eyes were still glued to her book.

"Okay," I said in an irritated tone and went towards the book rack.

I was not annoyed because she asked me to read a book; in fact I love to read. But the fact that she had ignored me continuously was kind of annoying. I took a book and started reading. 45 minutes later I began feeling sleepy as I had had a long day at work. At 9:30 pm I got out of my chair and put the book back in the rack.

"Shall I leave for the day?" I asked Namrata.

Finally she closed her book and turning towards me said, "Yes, sure you can. Tomorrow rehearsal will be from 12 noon."

"Fine, thank you." I left the rehearsal hall and headed towards my car. Namrata was leaving at the same time. I had no idea when the rest of them in the hall would come out of their private world to rejoin the real world and make their way home.

I was reversing my car out when I switched on the headlights and saw Namrata standing under a tree in heavy rain. Well, one thing I must say about Namrata, she was very beautiful. I would have surely fallen in love with her had I met her few years ago and if she had been closer to my age.

"Hey Namrata, please get in" I shouted cracking open the window of my car.

"Hey, thank you - my husband is so stupid I tell you," she said as she climbed in. "I told him to pick me up at 9:45 pm from the rehearsal hall but see how irresponsible he is? He doesn't care about his wife, stupid fellow!"

Now I saw a totally different character from the one in the rehearsal hall. I saw her in the role of a wife. While I was observing her, her phone rang.

Without even a 'hello' she said: "You are such an irresponsible man you know, duffer, idiot, stupid! You are a fool of the first order!" She added a list of abuses in some other language which I was not able to identify, but I was able to make out that she had attacked her poor husband - left, right and center.

"Is everything fine?" I asked when she hung up.

"Yes, the stupid fellow will reach in another two minutes," she said.

"Okay," I said, "are you from Punjab?"

"No, I am a Tamilian," she said.

"Oh I wouldn't have thought so, you are so fair," I said and immediately wondered if she would be offended.

"Are you trying to say Tamilians are not fair?" I was desperately regretting my stupid statement.

"No, I mean you are very beautiful," I stammered and thank God, that very moment her husband's car arrived.

"Your husband, Namrata," I quickly pointed out.

"Yes I know. Well, thank you for giving me shelter and waiting for my husband," she said and got out.

As it was raining heavily there was so scope for interacting with her husband. She just opened the car door, climbed in and left.

A few minutes earlier I had been admiring her beauty and envying her husband, but after glimpsing her temper I was quite put off. I could never be with someone like her. No wonder people say looks can be deceptive. Once again Hinsa came to mind. I realized that her looks were deceptive and had made a fool of me.

I sat silently in my car outside the rehearsal hall, lost in flashblack. After ten minutes I shook myself out of it and set off for home.

I was almost there when my phone started ringing, I thought it was a call from my mom, Arvind or Surjeet but when I saw my screen, I surprised to see the name flashing on my mobile.

"Hi Silvana!" I shouted.

"Hi Mr. Banana Babuna, how are you?" Both of us had a hearty laugh.

"I am good. How are you?"

"It's been quite long so I thought I should call you. Hope everything is fine at your end."

"It's all good, so when are you planning to come to India?"

"Don't know yet, but I will definitely try to come in the near future," she said.

"Are you serious? That's a great news do come fast. Have you called Arvind and Surjeet?"

"No not yet. You are the first one to I called. I will call them too, but not today as I am going right now to a friend's birthday party."

"Okay great. Plan your visit to India soon," I said.

"Sure. I'll will try to come soon."

"Silvana?" I said hesitantly.

"Yes, tell me."

"I miss you… and I miss the London nights too."

She was silent for a couple of beats then she said, "You are really a sweetheart Nekman. I miss you too dear."

It is so strange some people who are so close to you hurt you badly, which you could have never expected, whereas some people who are new in your life, give you love, affection and healing, unexpected from them. I realized this after talking to Silvana that night. She was new in my life but still, talking to her brought positive energy and happiness to me. Well, such is life! That's why there is a saying - never expect anything from life, whatever you get, cherish it. Then you will always be happy and never disappointed.

16

Insomnia Nights

"Nekman!" I was standing at a railway platform near my house. I turned to see who had called my name and saw Hinsa standing behind me. My whole body started trembling the moment I looked into her eyes.

We both just looked at each other in silence. A teardrop rolled down my face while she stood expressionless in front of me. For a fraction of second she smiled at me then, suddenly, a male voice from somewhere said, "Hinsa, I love you." On hearing this, Hinsa ran towards the guy while I remained standing like a statue. I shouted out: "Hinsa, please don't go! Hinsa please don't go!" But she ran into that's guy's arms and everything went black...

"Brother what happened? Wake up, wake up!" a voice was saying in my ear. I jumped out of bed and realized it was 3 am. Joy had heard me shouting in my sleep and tried to wake me.

"What happened brother?" Joy asked. "Nothing Joy, just a dream. You go back to your studies. I'll have a glass of water and go back to sleep.

"Okay brother, if you need something, call me." Joy said.

I went into the kitchen and drank half a bottle of water. I was still affected by that nightmare. My body was trembling and my heart was racing at bullet speed.

I went back to bed and tried to sleep, but couldn't. I just tossed and turned. This was becoming a pattern with me after my engagement had been called off.

Well, that night my dream dashed all hopes in me that Hinsa would return. I had a strong feeling that she would never be back in my life. Yet, her reasons for stepping away from our relationship were unclear to me.

Finally I fell into a troubled sleep. From then on I had to deal with insomnia at least once in every ten nights.

Arvind called – he said he wanted to discuss something important with me. I went to meet him in the Graveyard Bar. Yes, it had been a graveyard long back till a businessman purchased the land and built a bar. The owner cleverly named it Graveyard Bar to attract the youth. When you're young, you like to be different and to go to unusual places.

It was almost six months from the day my engagement had been called off and these six months had been a roller coaster ride for me. I had had extreme amounts of fun, crying, shocks and insomnia. In six months, a lot of other things had changed as well: Surjeet got busy with his mobile store, Arvind was still searching for something to interest him and I was completely occupied with my office day to day activities. Although I had never wanted a 9-6 job, I must admit that my job helped me fight back at the worst time of my life. Everything was slowly falling into place; finally there was silence after all the hullaballoo of my engagement being called off.

That's what I thought, but I was wrong. The feeling that everything was falling in place was an illusion. The disasters that had happened in my life so far, were just a trailer - a lot more smashes were lined up for me that I had never imagined.

"Hey bro, how are you?" I asked Arvind. "How was your day?"

"It was all good Nekman, a very good day after long time," Arvind said.

"That's great, it means you have found what you want to do, if I am not wrong."

"Yes brother, I will tell you, first let's order a drink," Arvind said. "What will you have?"

"Risky whisky," Arvind said. "Boom!" I said, and ordered two double "risky whiskies"

"Is Surjeet joining us?"

"Dude I called him, but as usual, he's too busy with his mobile store," Arvind said.

"You're right! These days he is never available before 10 pm."

"Cheers!" Arvind said as our drinks arrived.

"So now tell me what you wanted to discuss."

"I am going to Dubai for two years."

"What??" I shouted. "Are you kidding me?"

"No I am serious. Listen, didn't I tell you I had a good friend in Dubai?"

"Yes, so what?"

"So he gave me a business proposal. I shared it with my dad and he has given me the green signal."

"It must be good if uncle is okay with the business plan," I said

"Yes, so now I am leaving for Dubai in the next 15 days and I will be there for at least two years setting up the business."

"Two years…" I said heavily.

"Yes," he said and both of us fell silent. Arvind was happy and even I was happy for him but unfortunately he had to go far away for two years, that was disturbing for us. On other hand, Arvind was in no position to lose this opportunity as he had been searching for something good for almost six months.

"Hey, where did you get lost?" I said, thinking that I should motivate him.

"Nothing brother, life is so unpredictable and puts you in such situations where you feel helpless," he said.

"Yes brother, I know that very well. But come on, it's just two years!"

"Yes."

"Hey have you told Surjeet about this?" I asked.

"No not yet", he said and as if on cue, Surjeet's number started flashing on my phone.

"Surjeet, dude there is good news," I shouted as I took the call.

"You and Arvind are together? Just rush to my place as soon as possible," Surjeet said.

"Hey, are you alright?" I asked, startled at Surjeet's tone.

"You guys just came to my place at once, don't ask questions, I am not in position to talk now. Please come soon, both of you," Surjeet rang off.

Wondering what trouble Surjeet was in, Arvind and I rushed from Graveyard Bar to Surjeet's house.

We reached his place and pressed on the doorbell continuously. Surjeet opened the door and let us in without saying anything.

"Hey fucker, what happened?" Arvind asked Surjeet.

"Nothing," Surjeet said.

"Surjeet are you insane? Both of us panicked and rushed to your place, now you are saying nothing happened?"

"Brothers…"he started and fell silent.

"What the hell? Speak up!" Arvind and I demanded.

"I am getting married in 15 days," he said. Arvind and I froze on hearing this.

"Are you serious?" I asked.

"Yes brother, are you serious?" Arvind also asked Surjeet.

"Yes brothers," he said in a panicked voice. Arvind and I just burst out laughing. We laughed till Surjeet started beating us both.

At 1 pm that night we were in Surjeet's room having whisky. We all were good and high – having lost count of the pegs long ago.

I stood and hugged Surjeet, "Brother, congratulations - may God bless you."

"Thank you brother. Now I want you two, to also to get married soon."

I laughed and said that I didn't want to ever get married – "enough for me!"

"Why are you talking like this?" Arvind said.

"Nothing dude," I said and to change the topic I asked Arvind to tell Surjeet about his plans.

"What plans?" Surjeet asked.

"Brother I am going to Dubai."

"Why Dubai? What will you do there?" Surjeet asked

"He has planned everything and uncle has also given him the green signal to do business in Dubai. One of Arvind's college mates lives there who has given him a business plan. He is going there to implement it. This fellow is leaving in another 15 days. Thank god you are also getting married in 15 days otherwise he would have missed your wedding." I was lying on a sofa in Surjeet's room.

"Whatever Nekman is saying, is that correct?" Surjeet asked Arvind.

"Yes brother, I am sorry but I couldn't come up with any other plan. I was not able to find anything that I really wanted to do but this business idea was exactly what I was waiting for, so I took the decision," Arvind said.

"Okay, your choice Arvind," Surjeet said and finished off his peg in one go.

"Surjeet come on, don't be upset," I got out of the sofa to lighten up Surjeet's mood.

"I'm fine - let him go and Arvind, I think it's better you leave before my marriage," Surjeet said.

"Hey Surjeet, stop it man. Arvind is also upset but he has to do something in life to shape up his career," I said.

"So? He can shape up his career in India also," Surjeet said.

"Yes, but for the past six months he wasn't able to find anything, so destiny planned something else for him. Surjeet even you are busy with your mobile store now - you too have done something of your own, similarly Arvind also wants to follow his dream," I said pouring another peg.

After my speech Surjeet was silent for five minutes, then said: "You're right Nekman." He turned towards Arvind and hugged him tightly and they both burst into tears. I joined them in a hug and we all cried madly. This was the first time since childhood that we had cried like this.

"Arvind you go, earn lots of money and come back soon," Surjeet said.

"Yes, at least before Surjeet delivers his first child," I joked and three of us smiled.

That night was a very emotional and heartrending chapter in our friendship. I got back home extremely intoxicated, but was not able to sleep as I was hurting inside. I was disturbed because of the two big bombshells that both of them dropped on me, in one single night. It was like being struck by two bullets. I was very unhappy and sad because both of them were the positive forces in my life that time and suddenly both were going away from me.

Arvind was going to Dubai so I knew that hardly any interaction was going to happen on a day to day basis. Surjeet was getting married and I knew that after marriage, I couldn't expect Surjeet to be the same fellow who had hung around with us since childhood - after marriage a lot of things change.

Another reason for my dejection was the marriage part of it. I was happy for Surjeet but at the same time a knife twisted in me as I 'flash-blacked' to my engagement. I cried a lot that night with all these thoughts on my mind. The last thought before I fell asleep was a hope that there were no more smashes lined up for me because I did not think I could handle any more pain. But unknown to me the Big Bang was yet to come.

17

The Big Bang

The big day came. We were all happy, celebrating the big day in Surjeet life. Yes, it was his wedding day. Hundreds of guests were invited. There were lights, music and lavish food - in short it was the typical big fat Indian wedding. As Surjeet was from a wealthy Sikh family, everything was extra lavish.

A number of beautiful girls were present at the wedding but my pocket was too small to approach such wealthy girls. I realized that there was no shortage of beautiful girls in our country, the shortage was in a boy's bank balance. As long as you don't have a good bank balance, you can't afford a beautiful girl.

If you have a good bank balance and status no matter how you look or what your nature is, you can get any beautiful girl.

"Hey Nekman," Surjeet's dad called out.

"Coming, uncle."

"Son, where is Arvind? I told him to get extra bottles of liquor because I don't want any shortage of liquor at the party - otherwise I will feel very bad," he said.

I smiled inwardly that uncle was not worried about food, decoration cr any of the other important things, but he was worried about the shortage of liquor. "Uncle, don't worry. I will make sure Arvind gets extra bottles of liquor," I said.

I tried Arvind number twice but his phone was busy. I thought he may have be stuck with some work as Surjeet's mom had given him four or five things to manage, while I had to manage everything at the hotel where the wedding ceremony was held.

"Cheers!" I said and raised a toast at the bar with Surjeet's uncles and a whole lot of cousins. We started the celebration with 'bottoms up'.

"Hey Nekman, one more round of bottoms up," one of Surjeet's cousin requested.

"Sure brother," I served another round. We all drank like fish and then rushed towards the DJ to dance. All of us were enjoying ourselves to the fullest and I was very happy for Surjeet. After a few minutes of dancing I went to the groom's room where Surjeet was getting ready.

"Surjeet you are looking awesome man," I said as I entered the groom's room.

"You fucker, don't lie to me," Surjeet was busy knotting his turban which is the most difficult part of a Sikh's, grooming.

"No brother, I mean it," I said.

"Seriously?" We smiled at each other.

"Nekman, give me a peg dude. I'm too nervous to go downstairs," Surjeet said.

"Are you serious? Feeling nervous?" I laughed at him.

"Shut up and give me a peg!"

"I knew you will ask for a peg, so here you go." I pulled out a Jack Daniels from a pouch. This was Surjeet's favorite drink. I poured a good 90 ml peg for him.

"Awesome brother, I love you," he drank whole peg neat, in one shot.

"One more Nekman," Surjeet said.

"Dude enough, only one for you tonight. It's your wedding day tomorrow brother, get some rest now."

"Okay, but hey, where is Arvind?"

"No idea. I've been trying his line for the last 45 minutes but his phone is busy. Anyway, you get ready fast," I said and went downstairs to the ballroom.

Surjeet's marriage was like a festival, everything was so colorful and bright like a fairyland. At the back of my mind I was thinking about my engagement and getting upset, but I pushed those thoughts away – why brood on the past and it was my best friend wedding after all, I should be happy for him. But as I told you my life was full of smashes and in five minutes the biggest smash that would change my life, was heading my way.

'Tring, Tring.' My phone rang. It was Arvind.

"Hey dude, what the fuck? Where are you?"

"Coming brother," Arvind said.

"How long will you will take to reach the hotel? I hope you are bringing the liquor bottles which uncle asked for."

"Yes."

"Hey what happened to your voice? Why so dull?"

"Nothing Nekman, I'll be there soon."

"Is something is wrong Arvind? What you are hiding? Tell me fast, you fucker!" I shouted.

"Hinsa…" Arvind uttered and my whole body trembled.

"What about her?"

"Nothing, she…"

"What?? Tell me Arvind."

"She is getting married in 10 days." Now this was the Big Bang for me. I went cold and frozen all over.

"To whom?" I asked in a voice choked with pain.

"An actor, he comes in some serial," Arvind said and that was the final knockout punch. I stumbled to my car in the parking lot and sat in it.

My mind was a big blank. I was so numb that I could not express a single tear. My body was shivering. My breath struggled in my chest. I felt like death. I felt overwhelmed and helpless, not knowing what to do next or how to react - that very moment I saw the pouch in which I'd stored the Jack Daniels. I took out the bottle and in one shot I finished more than half. I had always seen in movies, the dejected lover turning to alcohol, but only now I understood why the heart-broken need alcohol so desperately.

Soon I was completely drunk and in such a bad way that I couldn't make my way to the hotel from the parking lot. Arvind was continuously trying my line. I ignored his calls but he eventually found me in my car.

"Nekman are you mad? What are you doing? It's Surjeet marriage and look at yourself - you are not fit to enter the hotel. Please forget that girl now, she is nothing to you anymore Nekman," Arvind said.

I stayed quiet.

"Nekman come on, get up. It is my fault. I shouldn't have told you about her wedding."

With a lot of difficulty Arvind managed me to take me to the room where Surjeet was getting ready.

"Nekman, wake up dude!" He splashed water on my face.

Suddenly my eyes opened. I was still reeling from the drink. "I am fine," I said.

"What the hell 'fine'? Why are doing this?" Arvind said.

I kept quiet for a minute and then the volcano within, which was I suppressing exploded. I sobbed and hollered my frustration. Watching this, Arvind panicked and tried to console me. Meanwhile Surjeet came in.

The moment Surjeet entered in the room he came straight up to me and caught me in a hug.

"Surjeet, it's all over brother," I wailed.

"No problem, it will get better brother, please don't cry," Surjeet tried to console me.

"Yes Nekman, we are with you. Don't get so upset," Arvind said and hugged me.

"I know, but right now please do me a favor - please call Hinsa or any of her friends, I want to talk to her just one last time. Please Arvind, Surjeet, please contact her."

"Okay wait, I'll call, don't panic," Arvind said.

"Surjeet you go downstairs. I don't want to spoil your wedding day - give me 15 minutes. I will come down with Arvind," I said.

"No. I cannot leave you like this."

"Please go, for the sake of our friendship. Please Surjeet. I will be right there, just 15-20 minutes is all I need to freshen up and have just one last word with Hinsa," I said.

"Yes Surjeet, you go. I will bring Nekman," Arvind said.

"Okay brothers. Please come fast," Surjeet said.

"Hey Rimi, I am Nekman's friend Arvind. Please listen to me carefully. Nekman is not in a good condition after hearing about Hinsa marriage. He just wants to have one last word with Hinsa and I need her number. Please it is a humble request to you. Kindly give her number or put her on a Con-call as Nekman is really desperate."

"Nekman, Rimi is putting Hinsa on a Con-call," Arvind said.

"Okay give me the phone," I said. "Hello? Hello Hinsa?"

"No I am Rimi on the line. I am sorry Nekman I had a word with Hinsa and she made me swear not to put you on a Con-call. She says she doesn't want to talk to you."

"What? What the hell does she thinks of herself? She doesn't want to talk to me one last time also?"

"I am sorry Nekman," Rimi said.

"Rimi please try and get her to talk to me. I am on hold. Please put her on Con-call," I pleaded.

"Okay I will try again Nekman."

I never thought in my wildest dream that to talk to her one last time I would have to plead so much. I was waiting on hold and my gut feeling was telling me that she would definitely come on call.

"Nekman?" Rimi released me from hold.

"Is Hinsa on the line?" I asked.

"I am sorry. She is not ready to talk to you. Please take care of yourself," Rimi said and hung up. At that moment I was just speechless with tears in my eyes, wondering again and again how Hinsa could be so heartless.

"Arvind she doesn't want to talk to me one last time also...Why? Am I so bad? Was my love so weak?"

"No Nekman, your love was not weak, it's just that her love for money is stronger."

Nothing was left in me, no emotions, no love, no happiness. I had made Hinsa the center of my universe and now I was being punished for it.

That night was the point when I began to slide into depression.

I took medicine so that I could go down and be normal for Surjeet's marriage. I tried to act as normal as I could though I was devastated, but it was Surjeet's marriage and I didn't want to spoil it. I managed to put on a happy go lucky face, but inside I was shattered.

18

Black Bubbles & Chocolate Cookies

I was still alive. I thought I would not survive that night, but I did.

News of Hinsa's marriage came as a big shock to me and it took some time to sink in. It was like a bad dream, but it was no dream. It was hard, black and white reality that I would have to accept, sooner or later.

Till now, I had refused to accept that Hinsa had done all this for money, but now I was forced to believe it as her new groom was bloody rich and the icing on the cake was that this soon to be better half was an actor – something which was my dream!

I woke up to the hard fact that in this Materialistic and Digital world, emotions had no currency, the only things that mattered for most people, were hard cash and possessions.

After Hinsa's marriage was fixed, it wasn't about her anymore. It was now all about me and the black future which stretched ahead.

Dismissing the deep thoughts flooding my mind, I got up to get ready. I had to drop Arvind at the airport for his flight to Dubai, the very next day after Surjeet's marriage.

My whole family were upset when they heard the news, and one person who took it equally badly was my mother.

"Mom, I'm leaving for Arvind's house," I said in a low voice.

"What time will you be back?"

"In some time," I mumbled. I tried to put on a brave face in front of mom, knowing that she would suffer seeing my pain.

The moment I exited the parking lot, tears began rolling down uncontrollably. On the radio, Hinsa's and my favorite song by Westlife was playing, which she used to dedicate to me.

> "I wanna grow old with you
> I wanna die lying in your arms
> I wanna grow old with you
> I wanna be looking in your eyes
> I wanna be there for you
> Sharing everything you do
> I wanna grow old with you"

I cried all the way to Arvind's house.

"Hey Arvind, come downstairs, I'm waiting for you."

Surjeet obviously couldn't come as he had just got married the previous night. Arvind and I knew that his life was now going to undergo a three sixty degree change and he would not be able to give us the same amount of time as before. Quite natural, now that he was a family man and no longer a bachelor.

"Hey Nekman, how are you?" Arvind asked as he got in.

"All good. Have you taken everything?"

"Yes don't worry, I've taken everything."

"Okay, that's great,"

"Nekman?"

"Yes?"

"Are you okay?" Arvind could make out from my face and eyes that I was disturbed.

"Yes Arvind, I am fine and if not, I will be fine in a day or so."

"She was not good for you Nekman, she was too greedy."

"Arvind let's not talk about her. Leave it. It is all my destiny and I have to deal with it."

"So when is Surjeet leaving for his honeymoon?" Arvind asked.

"Next week, I think. Hey, we've reached the airport."

"Nekman shall I cancel my flight and stay back for few days? Surjeet will also be gone for a month and you will be all alone," Arvind said.

There were tears in my eyes because Arvind and Surjeet were the people I was closest to, with whom I used to have a good time, cheering myself up. Unfortunately both were leaving, that too together, while I was going through the worst phase of my life..

"Are you mad? I am all good, don't worry brother. You go and make a big success story of yourself in Dubai," I said.

"Hmm…"

"Hey I'm seriously good. Now get going or you will miss your flight."

"Okay, I'm going but promise me that you will stop thinking of her and upsetting yourself," he said.

I smiled. "She is nothing to me anymore Arvind, but the memories are there and frankly speaking I don't know long it will take to erase them. Still, I promise to try to erase them completely.

"Okay brother," he hugged me.

"Take care and call me after reaching Dubai, okay?"

"Sure," he said and went inside to check in.

I got back into the car with tears in my eyes, feeling that everyone was going far away from me. I just could not accept that so many things were changing in my life.

Hinsa gone, Arvind gone and Surjeet also, partially gone. I was completely depressed and I had lost all faith in God. God had put me in extreme pain. I was in a dark tunnel with no hope of light anywhere. I didn't know it then, but the tunnel was going to get even darker.

I was on my way back after dropping Arvind at the airport when I spotted a big liquor shop. I was so frustrated and depressed that I parked outside the shop and went in to pick up some alcohol, even though it was just 3 pm.

"Can I have one quarter of 100 pipers whisky?"

"300 rupees," the shopkeeper said.

I reached for my wallet and realized that I had forgotten it. Then I checked for loose change in my pocket and found two 50 rupee notes.

"You want to buy something or not? Don't waste time," the shopkeeper said.

"You have something for 100 rupees?" I asked.

"Yes, rum. You want it?"

One of my father friends who was in the army, used to make a statement that stuck in my mind: he used to say, 'RUM is not alcohol it is a Regular Usable Medicine'. Remembering this, I told the shopkeeper to give me one quarter of rum.

The quarter of rum cost seventy bucks and I purchased a bottle of coke for thirty bucks.

I made my first peg pouring the black bubbles in 60 ml of rum and started drinking. I was hungry – I hadn't eaten anything since the previous night. I found a pack of chocolate cookies in the car. No one eats cookies with alcohol, so I am probably the first on this planet to try this combination for lack of choice.

I never thought that a combination of black bubbles and a chocolate cookies would give me such a high. That was a D-day for me, when I started on rum with black bubbles and chocolate cookies. From that day onwards I became a drunkard because it was the only thing that gave me relief from all the bad thoughts chasing around in my mind.

People say alcohol is bad, but for me, at that time, alcohol was my savior. I know it doesn't remove the pain but sometimes all you need is to suppress your pain.

That was the first half of my story. Let's see where life took me in the second half

19

The F world

"Nekman get up, RT is coming to our bay," Sonupriya shouted by my head. It was 10 am and I was fast asleep with my head on my desk.

"Let RT go to hell."

"Don't forget that Raman Thakur (RT) is our organization's vice president Nekman, now wake up!"

"You can go to your cubicle. Don't worry I am not in sleep mode now."

I was sleeping at my desk in the morning as I was drunk last night. It was two months since Surjeet's wedding and Arvind's departure to Dubai. In between, Hinsa had also got married. For the past two months I had made a great habit of rum, black bubbles and chocolate cookies, due to which, every second day I used to come to office with a hangover and sleep at my desk.

In these past two months my parents were very upset with my drinking; my performance in office was almost zero. My life was all dark and black like my drink. I was no more in love with life. I was just living for my family, that's it.

"Nekman, come into my cabin," Raman Thakur came to my seat and said.

"Yes sir."

Well, by now I was used to smashes and I was aware that another smash by Raman Thakur was waiting for me in his cabin.

"Sir, may I come in?"

In in his most authoritative voice he asked me to enter.

I entered the cabin and sat quietly. I was not nervous as the effects of last night's binge still lingered. When you are hungover or intoxicated, you are Mr. Prime Minister in your eyes. I waited quietly while Mr. Thakur attended to something on his Apple laptop.

Yes, I must mention Apple because it is one brand that every one aspires to have and in our organization, all those at the Director and Vice President levels got to use Apple laptops.

Mr. Thakur's room was neat and clean. The interesting thing about his cabin was that everything was white. Not only the wall paint but even his bag, chair, desk, lunch box, bottle, coffee mug – all white. The reason for this was that he was fascinated with the color white, and he always wore a white shirt too. Even I used to wear white shirts - not because of Mr. Thakur, but by chance even I loved the color white, though not to the extent that Mr. Thakur did.

Ten minutes went by and I had finished viewing everything in his cabin when suddenly he said, "Nekman."

"Yes sir."

"How you are doing?"

"Good sir."

"It doesn't seem to be."

"Why sir?"

"You know the answer to that yourself."

I kept silent.

"Nekman, look I hardly give time to anyone like this. You know I have the workload of the whole office on my shoulders, but as you are a management trainee in our organization, we want to give you a platform through which you can grow in your professional life - that's why I planned this deliberation with you.

Management trainees are like new born babies for our organization and we want to nurture our babies effectively and efficiently. For so many years our organization has successfully nurtured all management trainees, but this is the first time in our history that a management trainee is falling short," he said and stopped.

I kept looking at him in my hungover state, nodding along with every single word he said.

"I had a word with Pranav and Suraj and they have told me that you are going through a bad turmoil after your engagement was called off, but Nekman, you have to channel your energies in the right direction now.

It's high time you left the negative state of mind. I just want to ask you how we can help you or you tell that what you want to do, because if your performance keeps deteriorating like this, HR will surely give you a pink slip at the end of the financial year." He sipped from a glass of water.

"I know sir," I said.

"Then what?"

"Nothing."

"What do you mean by nothing?"

Again I said nothing, I was still badly hungover and everything he said was going like a bouncer over my head.

"Okay Nekman, if you don't know, then I will tell you what I want from you."

Blah, blah, blah… he droned on for the next fifteen minutes while I struggled to keep my eyes open. I was lucky that he didn't catch me sleeping with my eyes open.

"Nekman, are you are fine with this?"

"Nekman!" he shouted after getting no response from me.

"Yes sir, I am listening. I have understood everything. Thank you so much sir, for all your guidance," I said humbly, as if I had paid attention to each and every golden word of his.

I felt so relaxed after coming out of his cabin and drank a glass of water. I was feeling too thirsty.

"Hey Nekman, what did boss tell you?" It was one of my colleagues who used to be in competition with me. Did he really think I was unaware of that?

"Nothing," I said.

"I know! You don't want to tell me because you want to beat me in the next appraisal," he said.

"Nothing like that."

"Then tell me what boss told you."

I stared at him for ten seconds then said: "Boss is very happy with the way I'm performing and he wants me to go Singapore next week for a big conference, okay?"

"What??" He said and his balls were out of his pants.

"Yes, but please don't tell this to anyone out here," I said.

"Okay," he said with sweat on his face.

"Listen, I think you also deserve a trip outside India," I said.

"Are you serious?"

"Of course! You are more capable than me, plus you are an engineer too. I think Mr. Thakur is underrating you."

"Yes, you are right Nekman."

"So now go and tell Mr. Thakur that you are more capable and that you deserve an international trip," I was enjoying myself thinking of RT's reaction.

"Yes Nekman, you are right, I am going!" He said aggressively.

"Yessss! Go my bull and hit hard."

He went towards RT's cabin and within two minutes I could hear RT fulminating in a loud voice and I laughed to the fullest.

"Nekman, why can't you smile and laugh like this always?" Sonupriya asked.

I became silent as I realized I had laughed after a very long time.

"Hey what happened? You were looking cute, stay that way," Sonupriya said.

"Yes I will," I smiled.

"Sounds like that guy is having good time in RT's cabin," Sonupriya said.

"Yeah right," both of us burst out laughing.

At 7 pm in the evening all were leaving work and even I was done, but it was too early to go to the liquor shop - my drinking routine was from 9 pm - 12 pm, so I thought I would hang around in office for a while.

The office was almost empty and only I was there with a few colleagues, security guards and pantry boys.

I went to the pantry for a hot coffee and settled down to surf. I logged into the F world (the Facebook world). The first profile I searched for was Surjeet's, as I wanted to see his honeymoon pictures. Then I saw a few of Arvind's Dubai pictures which showcased the amount of fun he was having outside of business. After 45 minutes I thought of leaving.

Suddenly Hinsa came to mind. After her marriage two months ago, I hadn't tried to access her profile, because I knew it would be hurtful. She had married a rich brat who acted in TV soap operas and enjoyed some recognition/. After marriage, Hinsa's face too had frequently appeared in magazines and newspapers. I use to get frequent updates about her though I never wanted any.

On that day I opened her profile. Seeing her pictures triggered the usual turmoil in me. I was filled with a familiar concoction of anger and tears. I cursed myself for opening up her profile. After seeing photographs of her marriage and an article with her hubby in B-Town magazine, I felt frustrated and banged my laptop shut.

I sat numbly for few minutes thinking that she seemed so normal while I was the dumb ass in so much pain.

"Sir, do you want something?" one of the pantry boys asked. Usually they don't bother but probably he must have seen my eyes filled with tears.

"No thank you."

I left my office for my black bubbles and chocolate cookies. After seeing Hinsa my mood was blown and it was going to be an overnight session of black bubbles for me. To be continued the F night...

20

The F Night

"Can I have one quarter rum?" I had reached the liquor shop near my office.

"70 bucks."

After taking the quarter from him suddenly my mood changed and I gave him back the quarter with another 70 bucks for a half bottle of rum. The pain of browsing through Hinsa's profile required half a bottle of rum, whereas I usually only had a quarter.

"Sir, please decide what you want," the shop keeper said harshly. They are frustrated as they have to sell drinks till late at night and deal with all sorts of drunkards, realizing this I excused his harshness. "Sorry for the confusion, give me half bottle," I said.

"Your bottle sir," he handed it over.

By 10 pm that night, I was 5 pegs down. I was very high and all alone. I went to Connaught Place in Delhi, thirty minutes from home.

I just drove and drove. I didn't even know what I was going to do after reaching Connaught Place. Meanwhile, I thought of calling Arvind.

"Hello?"

"Nekman?" Arvind asked.

"How are you?"

"Great, my brother," Arvind shouted, "and you?"

"Doing great, just having drinks with my office colleagues," I lied as I didn't want to upset him by telling him about my actual state.

"Great man! Keep it up. Hope some good corporate chicks are also there with you."

"Yes dude, there are some good chicks," I said, his 'corporate chick' comment made me smile even in my black mood.

"Great brother! Listen, I will call you back in a while, I'm heading for a meeting right now," Arvind said.

"Okay, no problems," I said. "Arvind?"

"Yes bro?"

"Miss you."

"Miss you too brother. Are you are okay?"

I took a minute to answer him." Yes, I am fine and now you go for your meeting. Give me a buzz when you get free."

"Sure brother," Arvind hung up.

I kept on drinking in my car bar on the roads of Delhi and finally stopped at Bangla Sahib Gurudwara in Connaught Place and went inside. It was 1 am. I had no plans of going back home and was too high from my half bottle rum.

I really don't know why I thought of going to a temple, that too after drinks, but it seemed like a good idea at that time. I was frustrated and filled with anger and somehow I thought God was to blame for making my life hell.

I went inside the Gurudwara and instead of going into the inner temple I sat near a pond on the premises. Every Gurudwara premises contains a pond, big or small. Near the pond a group of Sikhs were chanting God's name in a song that was just amazing and soul soothing. I kept listening to that scng till it was infused in me. After a good 30 minutes the song came to an end and I opened up my eyes realizing that in the past 30 minutes not even a single worry had entered my mind.

That day I realized the magic of prayer - sitting there I was able to feel the peace, the purity, the calmness, the light of hope and the essence of oneself, the essence of being Nekman. I spent lot of time sitting there, feeling relaxed.

I came back home and it was 3:30 am. I was about to open the gate using the duplicate keys when I noticed that the lights were on, mom and dad were still awake.

"Mom?" I said as I enter the home and saw that they were both sitting in the drawing room.

Mom came up to me, slapped me and started crying.

"Where were you Nekman? We were continuously calling you. Just check your missed calls. Do you know worried your mom was?" dad said in anger.

I checked. There were 78 missed calls from my mom's phone.

"I'm sorry, I was stuck at work."

"Shut your mouth Nekman! Look at yourself and what you're turning into. There's no need to lie. Your mouth is stinking with the smell cf alcohol," mom wept. I kept silent.

"What the hell do you want to do with your life Nekman?" dad asked.

"Nothing."

"What nothing?" mom said.

"Nothing."

"Nekman, my son, I know you are upset because of Hinsa but now please close that chapter. Life goes on. Don't ruin yourself. We know for the past two months you are drinking every day. See what you're becoming! These drinks will lead you nowhere and destroy you."

"I know," I said.

"Then why do you drink?" dad asked.

I said nothing.

"Nekman," mom sobbed.

"Mom please don't cry. Can I go sleep now?" I went to my room.

As I lay in bed I thought: "Why am I giving so much pain to mom and dad? Instead I should kill myself." But I also knew that was not a solution. I still had some hope that something good would happen and I think this hope was all due to my mother's prayers which were keeping me alive.

One thing I felt after seeing the tears in my mother's eyes is that the pain your mother can feel for you, no one else in this universe can feel.

I fell asleep with one last thought – today, I may be making my parents cry but someday, I'll make them proud.

Making my parents upset was the last thing I had ever wanted to do but I was so frustrated after my break up with Hinsa and the way my career was going, that I had been pushed into behaving like this.

21

Lights, Camera and Nekman – II

Mr. Thomas: "Colonel your wife is having an extramarital affair, do you know?"

Colonel: "Mr. Thomas do you know what you are saying? And how can you be so sure. Just tell me name of that person and I will kill him."

Mr. Thomas: "No I will not tell you… because I don't want to be killed so soon!"

Colonel: "What??"

Another day at my theater class. I was simply sitting around watching the other artists who were performing the above roles. I was very disappointed with my theater classes because every time the director only wanted me to me to sit and observe the others performing, which was too frustrating. Every weekend I was devoting my time to theater. After working five days in the office, just to sit and observe without participating, was very frustrating.

"Namrata, I am pissed off sitting idle. Please give me some character to play," I said to my director.

"I have already told you, please sit and observe," she said.

"But I want to do something; sitting idle is getting me nowhere. I want to see myself on the big screen one day."

She laughed at me and said: "Then you are at the wrong place Nekman. If you really want to see yourself on screen, you should go for serial or movie auditions. Theater is an art which demands a lot of patience and passion."

"Yes, I think you're right."

"So now choice is yours."

"What choice?"

"Do you want to be a theater artist or not?"

I stayed silent for two minutes and asked myself: "Is this what I want?" After two minutes of cogitation I realized that I didn't want to be a theater artist.

"No Namrata. I don't want to be a theater artist."

"Great! Nekman, do you know why I always asked you to sit and observe other people?"

"No, I don't know."

"Because I knew this is not what you want from life."

"How did you know that?"

"Because if you really wanted to be a part of theater, you would have not felt frustrated while observing, instead you would have enjoyed it."

"Thank you for your time," I said, "I think I need not waste any more time here, instead I should search for what I really want to do."

"Yes Nekman and my blessings are with you, one day you will definitely achieve something." I was both touched and motivated by her words.

"Yes Namrata, I will surely make it to the big screen one day and you will see me," I said and left the rehearsal hall.

After coming out I sat in my car and reflected on what I really wanted to be. While I was sure I didn't want to be a theater personality, I still wanted to appear on big screen as an actor. Also, I felt that I was more of a commercial performer rather than the artistic type.

I was still unclear about what I wanted to do but yes, I was relieved. At least now I knew what I didn't want. That day I realized that it's equally important for a person to be clear on what he doesn't want in life as much as what he wants, then things will correct automatically. From that day on, I planned to erase the things which I didn't want in my life so I could focus on what I did want.

My phone started ringing and the number appeared to belong to a telephone service provider like Airtel or Vodafone, so I didn't pick up.

After two minutes I got another call from the same number which also I ignored, and then I got a third call which made me angry -so I took the call with every intention of firing the caller left, right and center.

"Who the hell are you? I am busy right now. Don't you understand? I don't need a connection or your offers. For God's sake leave me alone!"

"Nekman?" A voice softly enquired.

"I'm sorry?"

"Nekman?" I realized the voice was familiar to me.

"Hi, this is Silvana."

Oh fish! It was Silvana.

"Oh God! I am so sorry. Silvana, it's you and you are in India!" I exploded, startling a passerby so much that she lost her footing. "Oh fish!"

"What's going on?"

"Nothing, hold on a second..." I went to give the woman a hand but seeing me approach made her even more nervous and she jumped up and ran away.

"So Silvana, tell me, how come you're in India? When did you came? And for what? I mean where are you are right now?" I asked her multiple questions in one go as I was so happy to know that she was in India.

"Calm down Nekman, I will tell you everything, but right now, I want you to reach Gurgaon as soon as possible. I'm right now in Gurgaon."

"Are you kidding me? Seriously? You are in Gurgaon? Silvana I will be there in thirty minutes."

"Great! I'll be waiting for you in Ambience Mall at the CCD coffee shop."

"I'm on my way!"

I was so excited that Silvana was in India. I jumped into my car and rushed to Ambience Mall in Gurgaon.

Once there, I went to the CCD coffee shop and waited. 15 minutes passed and there was no sign of her. She had called me from the hotel landline and didn't appear to be carrying a mobile.

"Nekman!" A voice came from behind me. I turned and Silvana was standing in front of me, that too in Indian attire. She was wearing a beautiful black kurta with white pajamas.

"Silvana!" I ran to hug her.

"How are you Nekman?"

"I am very happy today and not able to believe that it's you, standing here in front of me!"

"Same here, Nekman," she smiled and both of us hugged each other tightly for a minute.

"For how many days are you are?"

"For the next two days I am in Gurgaon, the rest I will tell you later. Now please take me to some good place, I'm starving!"

"Hey where would you like to go and what would you like to eat?"

"Any good place Nekman, where we can sit together and chat for hours," she said with a smile on her face.

"Want to go for a long drive?"

"Sure, but where to?"

"That's a surprise."

"Great, let's go!"

There was a liquor shop in the mall from where I purchased rum, that too a full bottle, because Silvana was also there to be my partner in crime. I also picked up some snacks from a food outlet as Silvana was starving. Then we left Gurgaon for my surprise destination.

By 9 pm we were on the highway.

"Silvana, please open the bottle of rum."

"Right now? In the car?"

"Yes girl, we are on a highway, no fear of police."

"Okay I will. But tell me Nekman, where are we going?"

"Don't worry, I'm not kidnapping you."

"I know but please tell me."

"No it's a surprise and we'll get there in three hours."

"Okay." She started pouring pegs in our glasses.

We drove on chatting and drinking.

"Hey Arvind is in Dubai but why didn't you call Surjeet? He might have joined us," Silvana said.

"No actually, he is away on his honeymoon. He's likely to be back next week, but then too I doubt if he'll have time. He's newly married and has to give his wife his attention."

"But surely he will make some time for friends. He can't be busy with his wife every day!"

"Let's see… shall I tell you something?"

"Yes, tell me."

"I miss Surjeet and Arvind a lot these days, especially when I am drinking in the car because every time, all three of us use to drink in car," I said and became a little silent.

She took my hand and said gently: "I can understand how one feels when the people closest to you are far away."

I just looked into her eyes the moment she held my hand, and felt something after a long time. What that was I couldn't say, but something was definitely there between me and Silvana.

"Silvana."

"Yes Nekman?"

"You are really a nice girl, I like you a lot."

"I know," she smiled. "One thing I must tell you," Silvana said.

"What?"

"I have not seen such a golden-hearted person like you in my life, I don't know why I am telling you this, but I felt I should."

After Silvana said the 'golden-hearted' bit we both just looked into each other's eyes for a minute. We were just lost in that look when a horn blared out from behind. Silvan jumped: "Nekman, please concentrate on the road!"

"Yes," even I realized the need for caution.

For two second we both kept quiet and then started laughing.

"Nekman, I will kill you, stop it and let's have 'bottoms up'", she said.

I smiled and agreed.

"Nekman how much further to go?"

"Close your eyes for five minutes."

She closed her eyes obediently. The reason I asked her to close her eyes was that we were about to reach our destination.

"Silvana."

"Yes Nekman, can I open up my eyes now?"

"Please do." She opened her eyes and was speechless.

"Nekman, am I dreaming or am I really seeing the Taj Mahal, one of the Seven Wonders of the World, in front of my eyes?"

"No it is not a dream, the Taj Mahal is in front of you."

Well I thought the Taj Mahal would be a great thing for Silvana to see as she was in India for the first time and Agra is only a 4 hour drive from Delhi.

"Nekman, thank you so much!" She hugged me tightly. She was so delighted and surprised to see the Taj Mahal.

It was 1 am at night. Silvana and I were sitting in the car at a point from where we could view the Taj Mahal in all its glory. Entry to the Taj Mahal is allowed only from 5am to 6pm.

We had to remain in the car till 5 am and that was no hardship for us, as were already high and we still had some rum to finish.

"Nekman, are we going to spend the whole night in the car?"

"Yes. You only said you wanted to chat with me for hours," I said with a naughty smile.

"Yes I did! Fine. Make me another peg."

"Silvana I don't think you should have any more, you will puke!"

"No. If I stop drinking, then you should stop too."

"Fine, have another drink." I was in no mood to stop. Silvana finished her glass in one go.

"Silvana are you crazy? This is rum not beer. You just finished the peg in one go!"

"Yes."

"Why?"

She put her white beautiful finger on my lips to shut them.

A trembling started in my body.

"Nekman," she whispered.

"Yes Silvana."

"Make me feel yours."

I looked at her with a question on my face.

"Please make me yours tonight. You know, in London, when you were sitting on the bench, crying outside the orphanage, I fell in love with you that very moment. I knew it was too early to talk of love then, so I kept my mouth shut and promised God that I would confess my love, if, in my lifetime, God would let me meet you again. You know, this is God's magic that today I am in India sitting with you," she poured out all her feelings.

"Silvana, you are so stupid you know," I kissed her forehead.

"Nekman, please come as close to me as you can, please…"

"But Silvana…" I was going to say something but she kissed my lips and shut me up. That kiss lasted a while. After a few minutes I pulled away. Then we both pushed our seats back and hugged each other to kiss again. In a fraction of a second I was all over her, kissing her chin, her cleavage and then lower down. In 30 minutes our clothes were off and we made love. She let me touch her and lick her all over which drove me crazy. I drove at her like rain on sand and fucked her hard, very hard and she asked for more.

That's how we ended up that night. I myself was not able to believe how close I got to her, sharing so much passion. I thought making love to her with so much frenzy was all my hurt and frustration coming through.

22

Love At Taj

It was 5:30 am. Last night had been sensual, sensational, emotional… no words could describe what happened between me and Silvana. Silvana was sleeping in my arms. I hadn't slept the whole night wondering if Silvana was expecting a commitment from me - I was dubious whether I was in love with her.

"Silvana?"

She opened her eyes – eyes, crystal clear, like a silent deep ocean.

"Silvana, it's sunrise, let's go see the Taj Mahal."

"No. I'm good right here in your arms. I'm exactly where I want to be." The moment she said this, I got even more nervous. I didn't want to hurt her at any cost, and I was confused about what to say just then.

"Silvana, but we came here to see the Taj Mahal. Get up, otherwise we will get late. We also have to leave for Delhi today."

"No I don't want to go back to Delhi or London. Let's stay here forever," she whispered looking into my eyes.

I was lost for words, once again drowning in the deep

ocean of her eyes. I started to kiss her again, then stopped myself. What the fuck was I doing?

"Silvana, let's go."

"Okay," she smiled and we went to see the Taj Mahal.

Seriously, I must say that if someone doesn't believe in love and wants to see physical proof – the Taj Mahal is it. When I was at the Taj Mahal I felt like failing, oops, falling in love again.

The Taj seemed to be coated with a fine blanket of pearls, as crystal clear as a mother's heart, and with a glow - as if kissed all over by fairies. We entered the Taj and Silvana was extremely happy looking around. We clicked lots of pictures and explored the monument's beauty to the fullest.

"Nekman, thank you so much. I can't express, how happy I am today. Thank you so much for this lovely surprise," Silvana said.

"What 'thank you', stupid? No' thank you', no 'sorry' between friends," I said, hinting that I was only a friend nothing more.

She smiled. "Only friends, Mr. Malhotra?"

Yes, my full name is Nekman Malhotra.

I smiled at the way she'd said 'Mr. Malhotra' and was not sure how to reply.

"Silvana, yes we are friends," I said.

She smiled again and said, "Okay."

"Nekman, please take me somewhere where I can use the washroom and also I am hungry. I want to eat something good."

I took her to a very famous restaurant in Agra where you get an awesome Indian breakfast.

"Nekman – water! Water! Water!"

"What happened?"

"It's so spicy Nekman. Water please!"

I laughed and poured her a glass of water.

"Now you know you can't live in India!" I declared, once again, hinting that she should not see a future with me.

"Why?" she asked innocently.

"Because you will have to eat this kind of spicy food every day."

"I can learn to eat it. I bet that homemade food will be less spicy than this restaurant food."

"Yes but…" I hesitated.

"Tell me."

"Nothing."

"Nekman, if you want I can eat all this food without water also," she declared.

"Okay, great! Then continue," I said and she started eating her meal without drinking water. Within minutes her eyes were streaming with tears. I realized that I was behaving badly, so I stopped her.

"Silvana, you are so stupid you know, please drink water now. I am so sorry," I said.

"Why are you sorry?"

"To make you eat such spicy food." I offered her a chocolate.

"Nekman," she said, taking the chocolate from me.

"Yes?"

"I love you," she said with tears in her eyes and this time the tears were not because of spice.

"Silvana…"

"Don't worry, I know you are not in love with me - that's what you've been trying to convey from morning," she said.

"No it's not like that. It's just that right now I am not clear what I want out of life and where I'm heading. There's too much happening in my life right now and I don't know when it's going to get sorted out. I don't want to drag you into my problems." I said what I had to say and left the restaurant.

Silvana joined me outside.

"Silvana, I am sorry."

"Now don't make me feel guilty by saying sorry. I feel your confusion, frustration and pain."

I nodded miserably.

"Hey, look at me," she said.

I looked at her.

"Please be alright. I'm with you on this. I will pray that you find what you want out of life, because only then I can get you," she smiled.

"Thank you for understanding, Silvana."

"Nekman, even after finding your goal, if you feel that I am not the one for you, I will not be disheartened," she said.

"Really Silvana, you are very nice girl."

"I know and I will always be in love with you. This was the first time my heart beat so loudly for someone." She kissed me on my cheek.

Then we hugged each other and shed a few tears. That was a deep emotional moment between me and Silvana. Two different countries, two different languages, two different souls but still something in common which had us both in tears.

Ten minutes later we set off from Agra and only then I started to wonder why Silvana had come to India in the first place.

"Silvana, sorry but I forget to ask, what brought you to India."

She smiled mischievously and said: "Stupid - that means you were all into me alright."

"No seriously, tell me why you came to India."

"Okay – let me inform you that your Silvana is now a TV presenter who is going to interview the famous, the intellectual and the celebrities of the world. I came here for a 7-day workshop in Mumbai."

"That's great news - but how did you make the leap from cab driver to TV presenter?"

"Well, with a part time job as cab driver, I was doing a media course and I got placed in one of the big news channels in London."

"Amazing! Well done Silvana. But, how come you are in Delhi?"

"My training starts tomorrow but I came to India early to meet you. Tonight I have a 1 am flight to Mumbai from Gurgaon."

I looked into her eyes and said: "You know, you are so stupid."

"I know, but now stop looking my eyes otherwise you will fall in love with me."

"Okay, I won't look."

Life is full of surprises I realized that day. You never know what's in store for you at the next turn in the journey of life. I never imagined that someday Silvana would come like this, that we would grow so close to each other and that she would say the words: *Nekman I love you.* I mean, it was all so unexpected and surprising for me.

At that moment I thought, why worry about the future when everything is so unpredictable. One should just go with the flow of life.

We went back to Silvana's hotel, she checked out and we headed towards the airport. I waited with her outside the departure gate to have a last few words.

"So?" she said.

"So," I said.

"I am going, stupid."

"Yes I know."

"Then?"

"Nothing."

"Nekman," she said in loud voice.

"Silvana don't go."

"What?"

"No - just go and do your training properly. See you soon on television," I smiled.

"Nekman..." she hugged me.

I was all choked up, a few tears rolled from my eyes and even her eyes were wet.

"Come on, go now!! Enough of crying," I said.

She hugged me one last time and whispered," I will be waiting for you, good bye, take care, Nekman."

My heart was all filled with crazy emotions. The moment she went in I burst out crying and went to my car.

I cried, yes, but I was very happy that I had spent such a lovely time with her. Heading home I picked up my usual quota of black bubbles and chocolate cookies.

23

The Last Puke

Silvana's visit felt like a dream. In one single night a lot of things had changed between both us. I didn't know whether I was in love with her. Also, I was not willing to analyze it; Hinsa had shown me that love was bullshit and I had no faith in it anymore.

"Nekman, wake up, you will get late for office!" mom shouted.

"Yes mom, give me ten minutes." I was in no position to wake up. The previous night I had doubled my pegs to overcome the sadness of Silvana's departure. I had a bad hangover and I was feeling all pukish. Mom hadn't enquired where I had spent the last two nights as she was aware that one of my London friends was visiting. Also, it had been the weekend.

With a lot of difficulty I managed to get ready without mom knowing that I had a bad hangover and I left for work.

"Nekman, you're due to make a presentation to Suraj, Pranav Mascarenhas and RT," Sonupriya said, as soon as I entered my bay. I was shocked.

"What you are saying?" I asked her.

"Yes, ten minutes back RT's secretary asked for you. He told me all of them are waiting for you in the boardroom."

"But what presentation??" I said.

"How I do know Nekman? But you'd better run to the boardroom."

I ran to the boardroom.

"May I come in sir?"

"Yes come in," Suraj said.

I entered the boardroom and found the three of them waiting for me. The projector was switched on, lights were dim and all three were looking at me as if they were waiting for me to state my last wish before facing the firing squad.

"Nekman, you are 15 minutes late for your presentation. We've all been waiting for you," RT said in a stern voice.

There was a big blank in my mind as to when this presentation was fixed and what I was supposed to do. I was searching my memory frantically and coming up with nothing. Moreover, I was not able to even stand properly in front of my bosses as my whole body was shivering from a bad hangover.

"You were given a task by Raman a few days, to make a corporate pitch in front of us," Pranav prompted.

"No sir," I said.

"I am not asking you a question, I am informing you that you had been given this task by Mr. Raman," Pranav said in an irritated manner.

"Nekman, you were in my cabin a few days back when I told you that I need a corporate pitch from you and that it would be your last chance to prove yourself, right Nekman?" RT said.

Then I realized that this conversation could have taken place when I was in Mr. Thakur's cabin a few days ago, struggling to stay awake.

"Nekman, please speak up," Suraj said in a loud voice.

"Yes sir."

"So, shall we start?"

"Yes sir," I said without knowing what I was about to speak as I had not prepared anything, what's more, my head was pounding with a hangover headache.

I walked towards the screen, already the presentation was set up by them, and I stood there completely blank faced. I thought I should open my mouth and speak something rather than stand there like a dummy. My head was blasting but I finally decided to open my mouth.

Ten, nine, eight, seven, six, five, four, three, two, one. I opened my mouth and puked all over the boardroom table. It was the first time in the history of our company that someone had puked in the boardroom. I saw some of the vomit particles splash over my boss' suit and then I blanked out.

That was my last puke.

"Get me bottle of glucose and a pouch of electoral," a nurse was saying when I eventually opened my eyes. Through a blur, I could see my mom crying on a sofa nearby.

They say that the purest relationship in the world is that of mother and child. When a child is in pain the best medicine and cure for that pain is mom.

The moment I opened my eyes I said 'mom'. My mom came towards me and hugged me. Yes, I had been admitted in a hospital after I had fainted in office.

"Why you drink so much Nekman?" mom sobbed.

"Your mom is right, why are you doing this to yourself Nekman?" RT said. I turned my face and saw my family, all my bosses and other colleagues were present.

"Nekman, your mom told us everything that you're going through. We know that after your relationship ended you entered a difficult phase of your life, but there has to be an end to this. You can't stay with this pain throughout your life, you must stop it," RT said.

"Yes Nekman, Mr. Raman is right and *you* are the one who has to do this, no one else can pull you out of this mess," Pranav said.

"For the sake of your family Nekman, please stop this. We are with you. If you need more time to heal, we will give more time. Don't give up on yourself like this," Suraj said.

All three of my bosses stood by me and that was something which I was not expecting from them. I was listening to their words but didn't know how to react or what to say as I was not ready to make any commitment right then.

"Nekman, get well soon. Take rest for a week and then join office", RT said.

"Sir," I said, "I don't want to come back to office." At this the whole room fell silent, including mom and dad.

"What?" dad exclaimed.

"You heard me," I said.

"Nekman, are you out of your senses? This is your job you're talking about, your bread and butter! What you will do without your job?"

"I really don't know. All I know is that this job is something that I don't want to do."

Once again my family, colleagues and bosses in the hospital ward fell silent.

"Nekman, all the best for your future. I know you will find something and be successful. Take care," RT said and left without a backward glance.

Everyone left, one by one. My room became empty, with only close family around. There is another very important aspect of life that I realized then – even if you have an enormous number of friends, relatives and colleagues in your life, they all leave at some point, except your family who is there with you till your last breath.

I had given my family another shock by quitting my job. I was not aware myself, of what I was going to do in the future. I had become a zero.

———∽∾∽———

24

The Lost World

A week passed. I recovered and was released from hospital. I no longer had a job. While putting in my papers I was happy that I did not anymore have to do something that I had no interest in. On other hand I was also aware that this world is all about money. To survive in this planet you need money - without which your existence is nothing.

'My baby shot me down bang-bang,' a song by the famous singer Nancy Sinatra remixed by DJ David Guetta was one of the biggest hits in the clubs those days. I was enjoying the music, sitting alone in a night club, sipping my black bubbles. All around me people were dancing, grooving to the DJ, and the digital lights were spraying like acid rain, burning and blowing everyone that night.

"Sir, excuse me…" the bar tender said.

"You are excused."

"Sir, the lady in the black gown, sitting at the right side corner table wants to buy you a drink - so what drink would you like to have?"

"90 ml of rum and coke and bring this drink to the table where the lady is sitting," I said.

I went to the lady's table and looked over her closely. She was in her mid-thirties. She was too hot to resist with lush green eye liner, lips topped off with cherry lipstick and scented with a heady perfume which could drive any man crazy.

"Hello madam."

"Hello hunk."

"In this planet where money is more valued than life, you are spending such an important thing on me, whom you've only seen a few minutes ago," I said.

"I like you, that's why," she shrugged.

"Okay. What else do you do besides splurging your husband's money? I am sure you are a married women," I said.

"Yes you are right, I am married but I don't take money from my husband. I am self-employed."

"Hmm. What you want from me?"

"Your time."

"Interesting. It seems that checking out boys in nightclubs is your passion."

"Passion is bigger than anything else in the world and *you* are my new passion!"

"Point taken madam, but I am your passion or obsession?"

"Both. I like young hunks like you," she said directly.

I was taken aback for a moment. I had heard about sexually frustrated housewives, it seems that had now met one of them.

"Your husband is not enough to give you pleasure?"

She smiled, "I want more than pleasure."

"Excuse me, sir…" It was the bar tender with my drink.

I downed my 90 ml peg at one shot while looking into the eyes of the mysterious stranger.

"Hey, you are all right kid," she said.

"Oh give me a break, I am not kid! I'm Nekman."

"Nice name."

"Sorry madam, I have to leave. I am not a male prostitute who will satisfy you – what's more you are married, please think of your husband," I said.

"So what if I am married?"

"Ridiculous!" I muttered

"Hey come on, let's have some fun."

"Sorry madam."

"Hey, I just asked for a few moments of time."

"It's disgusting, you talking to me like this - at least think of your husband who is working hard for you!"

"What do you know about my husband?"

"Not much, but you are cheating on him, that I know."

"I? Cheat on him? You're right, my husband does work really hard - he fucks hard a number of prostitutes day and night. Shall I give you the list? Shall I show you pictures of his lovemaking which I found on his mobile?" Tears rolled down her face.

I listened to her in silence. I realized that the world was full of problems but ultimately we had to confront these challenges and fight back.

"Madam, I don't know what to say about this, but will sleeping around with some other person, solve your issues?"

"No," she admitted.

"Then why are you doing this?"

"Then what should I do? You tell me."

"I think you should divorce him and marry someone else."

"What??" She was shocked. Yes, for an Indian, divorce is something shameful both for males and females; people are prepared to die every day rather than face getting a divorce, because of social pressure.

"You heard me right. Get a divorce."

"That's impossible."

"Ma'am, if your husband is cheating on you, rather than getting hurt every night you should take a divorce and start a new life."

"Are you kidding?"

"No I am serious, do it."

"I think I should leave; it's late."

"No, listen to me."

"Why should I listen? You're talking crap."

"Fine, become like your husband, then there will be no difference between you and him."

She was silent and swallowed her peg in one go.

"Madam, I am serious. There's no harm in getting free rather than dying of humiliation every day. I know that divorce is not easy in India, but ultimately you will feel good."

"I suppose you're right," she sighed.

"Yes, that's the spirit; you are independent woman. You earn your own living, if I am not wrong?"

"Yes sure, I am an investment banker."

"That's great! Then you should ask your husband for a divorce tonight!" My pegs were beginning to hit me.

"Yes, I think I'll do it! I will divorce him and be free forever."

"So, let's enjoy this night."

She called the bartender over and ordered ten 10 tequila shots on her credit card.

"But I don't drink tequila," I said.

"And I don't get divorced every day!" Both of us laughed.

"Bring it on, I am ready!"

"Cheers!" We were blown after the tequila and we danced to number of Bollywood tracks till 2 am.

"Hey are you alright?" I asked her as she vomited thrice. I was driving her car to drop her off, leaving mine behind.

"I am okay, you drive safely," she said woozily. I was also intoxicated but I managed to drive the car safely.

"Slow down, take a left for my apartments. We're almost there."

Finally we reached Marwaha Mansion, her residence.

"Your husband seems to be a rich man," I commented.

"Yes, but very poor at heart," she said. "He is the chief editor of big media group and he has plenty of ancestral property."

"Okay - maybe that's why he's a Casanova."

By then, it was almost 4 am. I got out of the car and went inside her house picking her up in my arms. I thought I should help her reach her bedroom.

"Are you alright?" I asked as I laid her down on her ultra-soft bed.

She dozed off while I was still sitting beside her, but when I got up to leave she grabbed my arm.

"Thank you," she smiled, holding my hand.

"For what?"

"For making me feel alive today," she said. When I heard that, I wondered how I could make someone else feel alive when myself I felt dead every day. The thought made me smile.

"Why are you laughing?"

"Nothing, just like that," I said, marveling once again at how I could be so good at counseling others, but when it came to myself I was drenched in negative energy!

"You're nice; I'm sure you'll meet someone wonderful."

She stood up to hug me farewell when suddenly someone hit me hard on my head from behind. Her shout was the last thing I heard before I lost my senses.

"Wake up you rascal!" I opened my eyes slowly and saw a police inspector and a gentleman in a black suit standing in front of me. After a fraction of a second I realized that I was lying on the floor at a police station, handcuffed.

"Wake up you son of a bitch, you gigolo, wake up!" the gentleman in the black suit shouted. He glared at me in hatred.

"Who the hell are you and why you are shouting at me?" I asked. This time my head hurt more from the blow than a hangover.

"I'm the one with whose wife you were having good time last night," the gentleman said.

That moment I understood the reason why I was lying handcuffed in a police station.

"Sir, don't worry, we'll make sure this guy learns a good lesson for what he did last night," the police man assured the gentleman.

"Mr. Marwaha, your wife is a very nice lady and we did nothing wrong. Please don't misjudge us."

"Just shut your mouth you rascal, don't lie! I will also make sure that I screw my wife's happiness now," Mr. Marwaha threatened.

I laughed. "Mr. Marwaha, how much more do you want to screw her happiness?"

"What you mean?"

"She is already aware of your sexcapades with prostitutes and dies of shame every day because of you."

"What the hell are you talking about?" he blustered.

"You, yourself know the truth and you are doubting her?"

"Inspector make sure this boy not only gets a good lesson but a hard one. I will handle that bitch," he snarled and left.

At that moment I felt very bad for Mrs. Marwaha - her cruel husband was going to make her even more miserable.

As for me, I had never imagined that someday I would land in jail - but what you think can never happen to you in your life, most often does. One should never think that life is under their control, instead one should welcome the surprises of life, good and bad with open arms - thinking this, I fell asleep in my jail cell.

———∽∼∾———

Jail trail

It was 8 pm and I was still in jail – wide awake and over my hangover. I had no idea if anyone had tried to reach me as my mobile had been taken by the police.

My first thought was to call home so that my parents could come and bail me out. On the other hand, hadn't I tortured them enough without giving them the additional shock of hearing that I was in jail? I dropped the idea.

"Dude, do you want to go back home or not?" the inspector came towards me.

I nodded in relief. Was he just going to let me go?

"Then tell someone to come to pick you up."

"Not bad," I thought, maybe after beating me so much the inspector does not want to demand anything more.

"But listen, whoever is coming, tell that person to bring ten thousand rupees."

Welcome to India! Now to get free from that jail I had to feed the inspector ten thousand bucks.

I started thinking about what to do next. Surjeet came to mind.

"Can I make one call from my mobile phone?" I said the inspector.

He asked one of the sub inspectors to let me out of the cell. I tried Surjeet's line.

"Hello Surjeet."

"Nekman! Where are you my brother? It's been so long, you never call me and don't take my calls," he said.

"Listen, I will tell you everything. Right now, I'm in trouble. Please come to South Delhi's main police station ASAP. I am stuck here."

"What???"

"Yes. Please come and bring ten thousand rupees with you."

"Okay," Surjeet hung up.

After my call, I was thrown back in jail. At 9:30 pm two more prisoners were put into my cell, one was in a black shirt and the other was in a white shirt. I was horrified to be locked in with real prisoners.

Hi, I said, tentatively. No reply. After a while, the one in the black shirt said hello.

"Why are you here? What's your crime?" he asked.

"Nothing, just a small misunderstanding," I said. "What have you done?"

After looking me over for two minutes he replied, "Murder". I quaked, realizing that I was sitting with a murderer.

"Yes, I am in here for murder and…" he pointed to the guy in the white shirt, "he is my partner in crime."

I was wishing now that I had not started this conversation. I just gave them a sweet smile.

"He doesn't like to talk?" I indicated the guy in white.

"No, he is mute. He can't speak and right now, he is depressed."

"Sorry to hear that. Why did you people murder someone?"

He looked at me and said, "I'm wondering if I should tell you what really happened."

"Yes, please tell me."

"Well it's not murder but a rascal's plan to swallow our property," he said. "We have a lot of ancestral property. Me and my younger brother..." he indicated the guy in white, "we live together. I'm single and didn't get married as I had to take over the business when our parents died.

A few months back my younger brother came home with a girl and the girl told me that they were in love. I was excited and happy that at least my brother had found his soul mate. Without a second thought I consented to their marriage."

He paused for breath, his younger brother who had been listening to us started crying. I waited for him to continue at his own pace as it was obvious that something bad had happened after their marriage.

The prisoner in black took up the story again.

"A few days back I came to know that the girl had married my brother to get her hands on our property. She was planning to get us both killed and get the property transferred to her name. She planned this dirty game with her brother."

"Oh shit!" I said.

"Yes. We immediately decided to file for a divorce but her bloody brother was too smart - he killed his own sister and made it look like we did it. Now if we are both sentenced to death by the court, the whole property will go to him, as we have no other close kin."

I was speechless to hear that this kind of shit also happened in life.

"Yes, but we are fighting for justice and I have faith that we will soon be freed," he said.

"I like your positivity and courage Mr. Black Shirt," I said.

"My name is Ranjeet," he smiled.

"Nekman!" A sub inspector shouted my name and said that someone had arrived to bail me out.

I was happy that Surjeet had come but right now, I was willing to spend more time in the jail cell with Mr. Black Shirt. If I had told someone that I was willing to spend time in jail, they would have laughed at me.

"Seems someone has come for your bail," Ranjeet said.

"Yes, I called one of my close friends."

"Boy, you seems to be a good soul. Anytime you feel like meeting me, please come," he said and gave me his phone number.

"Thank you Ranjeet. I hope you and your brother get out of this mess ASAP."

"I'm sure, we'll be free soon. God is there and he will never do wrong with anyone who's right," he smiled.

I shook hands with both of them and left the cell.

One thing which Ranjeet had said stuck in my mind: *God never does wrong with the ones who are right* - but I was not able to accept it.

"Nekman!" Surjeet shouted when he spotted me. "Are you alright?"

We hugged each other.

Surjeet paid up, I signed some papers and we both got out of there.

It was 11 pm by then, and I was feeling bad that I had called Surjeet so late and disturbed his married life.

"Nekman, what have you done to yourself?" Surjeet said, once we were on the road.

I was expecting this question from Surjeet as we were meeting after two months. In these two months I had been drinking regularly, I had lost 7 kgs, I had dark circles under my eyes from all the late nights and I had grown a thick beard.

"Nothing brother, I am fine."

"No you are not! What crap have you been up to? How come you landed up in jail?"

"Long story, I'll save it for another time."

"Nekman, Arvind and I tried to make you understand so many times, don't spoil your life for that bitch Hinsa. She is happy with her life and doesn't give a damn whether you are alive or dead. Then why the hell are you screwing up your personal life and career?"

At this, I smiled and told him that I'd quit my job.

Surjeet was so shocked he immediately pulled over.

"What the hell? Are you out of your mind? Have you really quit?"

Suddenly Surjeet's phone started ringing.

He took the call and I could hear a lady's voice raised in anger. I understood that it was none other than Surjeet's wife.

"I'm coming, don't shout. My friend was in trouble that's why I had to rush out so late."

I felt bad that I had caused a fight between Surjeet and his wife.

"Hey Surjeet, I think you should leave now - your wife sounds upset."

"Leave her. First listen to me. Please think of your parents and join your job again. You have the responsibilities of your parents on you Nekman," he said.

"Yes I know that. But I hated my work and it is better that I don't do something which I don't like."

"Fine, but then, what do you want to do?"

"Don't know."

"Oh! So when you will come to know what you want to do?"

"I really don't know."

He studied me for a minute and said, "I know, Nekman that your life has been affected a lot because of Hinsa, but please put it aside. You have your whole life in front of you. Also, whatever you want to do please decide fast and start doing it."

I nodded.

"I just want to see you happy."

"I am very happy and thanks for the bail." I got out of the car feeling annoyed.

"Where you are going?" he asked.

"Nowhere."

"I seriously don't know what is your problem is," he said.

I smiled and said, "I wish I could make you feel what I'm feeling now."

He was silent for a minute, then said: "Nekman I will pray that you get a good life partner and that you will soon find a career that will make you happy."

Surjeet had always had a definite career path, defined by his dad, I never expected him to be able to understand my situation by any chance. It was not Surjeet's fault, because everyone's story is different. Many will find my story confusing and full of surprises.

Most people want two things from life after adolescence: first, a good career and second, a good love life. Both these things in my life were destroyed, that was my problem.

My thoughts turned towards my mother after I stepped out of Surjeet's car and right enough my phone started ringing. Mom was on the line.

I felt happy to see my mother's call as this was the second night I was out of the house.

The moment I took the call I could hear my mom crying piteously. I knew something was wrong.

"Nekman, come soon, your dad is…" she sobbed.

"What happened mom?" I shouted, my heart racing.

"He's been hospitalized since last night, come fast," she said and every other thought went out of my head as I rushed to the hospital.

I never knew that the next couple of hours would be the worst in my life and they would change everything, in the same way that my broken engagement was a turning point. Also, I would like to say that it was good that those nightmarish hours happened, because this time, my life took a positive turn

26

Bad Hours

It was 1 am at night by the time I reached hospital. I came to know that my dad had been diagnosed with a kidney problem. One kidney was severely damaged which needed to be immediately removed, according to the specialists.

Mom was almost hysterical with worry, wondering what was going to happen. My younger brother was sitting there helpless, his eyes looking at me in search of some miracle, because next to dad I was a father figure for him - but those days I was more of a good for nothing wastrel.

The hope in my brother's eyes made me feel even worse about myself. "Hey, everything will be fine," I mumbled to Joy.

"I know brother, you are there for us. You are the best brother and son in this world," he said.

"No I am not," I said.

"Brother it's just that for a few months you have been disturbed. It's a question of time, soon you will be your old self." I marveled at hearing such wisdom from him.

"Take care of mom," I told him and left to see the doctor.

"Hello doctor," I said, "My name is Nekman, my father is in ICU with kidney failure."

"Ah yes," the doctor said.

"Doctor what is the next course of action? When you are going to operate?" I asked.

"We have started his treatment and the operation will be performed tomorrow morning."

"He will be out of danger after that?"

"Yes only one kidney is damaged so we will remove that. The human body can survive on one kidney without any problem," he said. I felt better after hearing the doctor state that dad would be out of danger after surgery.

"Thank you doctor." I took a deep breath and stood up to leave the doctor's cabin when the doctor called my name.

"Yes doctor?"

"One more thing," the doctor said, "You must deposit 20 lakh rupees by tomorrow morning and complete all the required paperwork."

My blood ran cold on hearing this. The doctor was not wrong, he was operating on my dad and the fees needed to be deposited in the hospital.

"Yes doctor, I will arrange the money," I said.

At that moment I realized the importance of money, which I had always ignored. My head was spinning in empty circles. I had no ideas from where I was going to source this huge sum.

I came out of the hospital and sat on a bench thinking of every avenue from where the money could be arranged. Suddenly I remembered one of my dad's cousins - he was quite wealthy and close to dad as well.

I pulled out the phone from my pocket and called my uncle, whose name was Bunty Chadha.

"Hello, who is on the line?"

"Uncle, I am Nekman here," I said.

"Hey Nekman, how are you son?"

"Uncle I am in a very bad situation. I need your help," I said and told him about dad's kidney failure.

"Nekman don't worry everything will be alright. Shall I come to hospital right now?" At once I felt relieved.

"Yes uncle please come and one more important thing - I need 20 lakhs. It has to be deposited in the hospital tomorrow morning. I will repay you as soon as dad gets alright."

"Nekman arranging 20 lakh rupees overnight will be impossible. I don't have this amount of money with me right now. Last week I lost a lot of money in the share market," he said. From his changed tone of voice I understood that he didn't want to give me the money.

"But uncle, can you at least arrange it through someone else?" I asked in desperation.

"No Nekman, sorry. But I will surely come tomorrow morning to see your dad. Good night," he said and hung up before I could say another word.

Now I really started panicking because he was the only rich hope I had. I had no clue what to do next. I did not want to call Surjeet and disturb him again. I could have called Arvind but I didn't see how he could help from so far away.

So I continued to sit on that bench, five minutes away from hospital, feeling helpless. My mind was blank and my hands were getting sweaty as the minutes ticked by and the time to make the deposit grew closer.

"Hey you," someone called me.

I looked around and realized that two thieves were behind me.

"What you want?" I faced them fearlessly.

"Money is all we want," they said pointing a gun at me.

"I have nothing, let me go."

"Don't try to fool us!" one of them said.

I was already very upset so I shouted and kicked out at which they both began beating me up.

I kept quiet for few seconds then started crying in front of them. Even the thieves were taken aback at the way I was crying.

"What happened?" one of them finally asked, as my sobs grew louder and more desperate.

I poured the whole story of my dad kidney's failure and my money crisis.

"So now what you are going to do to get money?" one of the thieves asked.

"Don't know," I said.

"You are going to sit on this bench and keep crying till morning?" Another thief asked.

"You people tell me then, from where I can get the money," I shouted.

"Come with us for a robbery."

"Robbery?" I looked at them with a big question mark on my face. "No I can't."

"Then how else will you get the money for the deposit by tomorrow morning?"

"But... robbery?"

"It's robbery, not murder," they said.

The thieves were right that sitting and crying on the park bench was not going to solve my problem. I began to think that maybe their suggestion was the only option left.

"Okay, but where and how we will rob?" I asked them.

"You don't worry about all that, just come along with us."

"Okay, I'm in," I said with courage born from desperation. That's how badly I needed the money.

Around 4 am the thieves bought me to a colony where the super-rich live. Their plan was to steal from one of the houses there.

We stepped into a house in that community. I should say 'bungalow' actually, because it was as huge as a palace, the kind only seen in movies. There were two security guards on whom the thieves sprayed something that rendered them unconscious. The bungalow was very huge with several rooms. The thieves pointed out one particular room to me and indicated that I should enter and steal whatever I could. They warned me to be careful as they knew there was a lady sleeping there alone.

"Hey, how do you know that only a lady is sleeping in that room?" I whispered.

"Boy, we are thieves and we plan everything before a robbery. We have watched this house for almost two months and that's why we came here tonight, because we know her husband is out of town."

"Okay," I breathed.

"Now, you go and do what you have to. Good luck!"

They were right. I entered the room and saw that there was a single lady sleeping on the bed. A small night lamp was switched on by the light of which I was able to see everything in room. I was not a professional burglar, so it took me some time to locate the money and jewelry. I searched desperately for five minutes till I saw a Safe to the left of the bed. I struggled to wrest it open but unfortunately I lost my balance and fell on the bed. The lady woke up and started to scream. I clamped my hand over her mouth.

Then I caught sight of her face and fell speechless.

"Hinsa," I murmured.

"Nekman!" For a moment we just stared dumbly at each other.

I stood up and moved aside.

"Well, well - so this is the palace for which you threw me aside," I said.

"Nekman, what are you doing here? she hissed.

"First answer my question."

"Yes! For this palace I left you. Anything else you want to know?"

I was taken aback by her shameless admission. "Well done, Hinsa!"

"Now, you tell me why the hell you are here!" she said.

"I came to rob you."

"What??"

"It's true." I didn't want to explain about my father; I knew now not to expect any sympathy from her. Much better to keep quiet.

"Oh, well done Nekman, now you have become a thief," she said.

"Yes I am a thief."

"Thank God, Nekman, I didn't marry you. My father was right about you and your family. You are good for nothing Nekman! If I had married you, you would have ruined me. You are such waster!" she spat.

I looked at her for two minutes and thought that this was the girl for whom I had been through so much and put my family through hell.

"I have no words for you Hinsa."

"I know you have nothing to say. You want money? Take it! My husband can afford it. We are not beggars like you. Tell you what - take this money as a tip from me for spending a few years by my side and never again show me your face."

"Yes I need money, I accept you offer."

"Yes Mr. Thief, go ahead."

I opened the Safe and helped myself to everything in it. While leaving the room my eyes stung with tears of humiliation, but pride was something I could not afford. What an unfortunate coincidence that it turned out to be Hinsa's house!

Each and every sentence Hinsa had uttered was burned indelibly into my brain. My tears poured out like a tempest but that was the last time I cried over her. Her words made me realize how important money was - she was right to call me a waster. That day I resolved to do whatever it took to become a rich man. I vowed to myself that one day I would return to Hinsa five times the amount that I had stolen from her.

Cogitation

What is Life? I asked myself looking at a wall clock in my bedroom but I was not able answer my own question. I was lying in bed a week after dad's surgery.

Dad was on medication, but on the mend. He was on leave from his office for a month. This was the first time my dad had ever taken off for such a long time. He was very particular about attendance and only took leave for dire emergencies.

Dad's crisis and the meeting with Hinsa made me re-think my attitude to life. In the recent past, after my engagement had been called off, I had let myself sink into depression, behaved badly, drunk myself senseless, quit a good job, spent time in jail and become a thief.

Somehow Hinsa's cruel words and the sobering effect of dad's operation, brought me back to reality. I had faced the worst and emerged stronger for it. After my dad's operation I promised to make something of myself and never be in a position where I was desperate for money. I knew that just dreaming of becoming rich would lead me nowhere, I needed a plan. Getting an idea in life is no big deal, the big deal is to execute that idea. The problem is that with even all the will in the world I still had no clue what to do and where to begin.

"Nekman," my mom called. "Son can you please go and get one big container of mineral water."

After the kidney operation as per the doctor's recommendation, dad had to drink only mineral water.

I was about to leave when mom called me again.

"Nekman," she said. "I've been wanting to ask you - how did you manage to arrange the money for the surgery?"

I had been dreading this. There was no question of telling mom the truth – it would have destroyed her.

"Nekman?" she asked again.

"Er…I took money from someone on interest mom. I will pay them back, don't worry," I said.

She searched my face for two minutes. She was the one who could easily tell from my face whether I was lying or not and she must have known that I was lying, but for whatever reason, she let it go.

I escaped to the market to buy mineral water.

I went to a big grocery store with many shelves, filled with products. To me, what was most exciting, was the ringing of the cash register. It sounded like a lot of money was being made.

By then my thought processes were consumed with making money. As I said earlier, this was my new mission in life.

"I will open a grocery store, yes, this is what I want to do," I said to myself and planned to dig out trade secrets from one of the employees of that store.

"Hey," I murmured to one employees standing around.

"Yes sir, what do you want?"

"Nothing, I need five minutes of time, if you can spare it."

He looked nervous at that and said, "Why sir? What happened?"

"Nothing happened, I just want to talk to you for few minutes outside the shop. What's your name?"

"Braham sir, but right now I am on duty. I can't come out of the shop."

"Okay. What time are you free?"

"Sir, seven in the evening."

"Okay Braham, I will meet you at seven outside your store, at the juice corner."

I immediately started feeling better now that I had a business idea to explore. I went home happily, thinking of all the questions I should ask Braham, after which I could open my own grocery store.

At 7:10 pm I was at the Juice shop outside the grocery store and I saw Braham heading my way.

"Hey Braham, how was your day?

"What's there to tell? It was as usual sir," he said dully.

"Hey, let's have some juice," I said.

"No sir, thank you."

"Please have one glass of juice - it will do you no harm," I said.

"Okay sir."

I ordered two glasses of mixed juice and I laughed to myself that instead of rum, I was asking for juice.

"For how many years have you have been working in this store?" I asked Braham, taking a long sip of juice from my glass.

"It's been six months since I joined this store."

"And how are the sales of this store?"

"Sir, sales are very good and the owner is also planning to open a new store soon." This was encouraging news!

"Great! So approximately how much profit per month does he take home?" I asked.

"Sir I don't know exactly, but I think it must be around 50 thousand bucks," he said.

"Okay."

"But sir, there is a lot of investment behind this 50 thousand buck profit."

"How much?" I enquired curiously.

"Sir, something like 20 lakhs on stock and every month the rent is 30 thousand…" already my motivation was evaporating as I was no mood to steal more money.

"Okay good," I said dejected

""Sir can I go - otherwise I will miss my bus?"

"Sure, you may go." I started heading towards my car, wondering what to do next.

I came back home deep in thought. Every business needs investment and I had no money to invest. Therefore I would have to look for a business that would require zero investment. The big question was, did any such business exist that required no capital as start with? Unfortunately I had to admit to myself that the answer was a big 'No'.

At 1 am that night my thought processes were still buzzing with the question of what business needed zero investment. I was not able to sleep so I switched on the idiot box and began surfing aimlessly.

After skimming through four scenes of a movie and listening to a couple of songs on MTV, I finally settled on a telemarketing channel where several new products were being demonstrated.

I listened to the spiel for a special type of milk meant for pets which, if the marketers where to be believed, would make pets obedient and active.

Then I saw a product that was mind blowing - a capsule that would make men pregnant! At this, I couldn't stop myself from rolling on the bed and laughing my sides out.

When I finally stopped laughing, I found that I was still wide awake. I continued surfing channels till I came across a food and travel show. A program named EAT CREATIVE was coming on, in which they were showcasing food joints that offered creative cuisine and provided a creative ambience for customers.

There was an interview with the owner, at the end of each segment, in which the interviewer asked them about the inspiration and approach behind their venture.

"Mr. Pillai, so what motivated you to open such an amazing creative restaurant?" the channel presenter gushed. I was watching one of the interviews with the owner of a restaurant in Chennai, South India.

"The one thing that motivated me to open such an innovative restaurant was my failure and depression," the owner of the restaurant said with a smile, and I was surprised to learn that a successful man like him had faced failure at some point in his life.

"Are you serious sir? What did you fail at that prompted you to opening this restaurant?"

"I was a big time player in the share markets and a stock broker myself, but unfortunately I lost my entire capital. With that, I also lost my nerve so that I could not play the big share game again."

"Didn't you miss the excitement of the share market and the prestige of being a stock broker?"

"Yes initially I missed it a lot and there were many circumstances when I wished I could be a stock broker again but I was in no condition to enter the markets, so finally I decided to be a restaurant owner - but yes, I still dabble shares, but in a small way."

"So how did you get started? What gave you the idea to open a restaurant specializing in 200 types of Idlis?" (Idli is a South Indian dish).

"Well that's an interesting story. Since childhood I had two passions: one was making money and the other was Idlis. When I was depressed after losing all my money, I thought - why not sell what I love? Also, this business didn't call for a big investment. I started with selling only one kind of Idli and today, by God's grace, I am selling 200 varieties of Idilis."

"That's great sir. Your life story is inspirational for many!"

Mr. Pillai laughed: "I have told you only a small part of my struggle and how I got here."

"Sir, that's just you being humble! Any words of advice for young entrepreneurs?"

"Work hard. Never give up. Never be satisfied. Always strive for more and keep exploring."

It was inspirational - especially for a guy like me who was lost and didn't know what to do.

After watching that I slept with a smile on my face, so motivated was I from watching Mr. Pillai's interview.

28

A Glass of Coke

The next day I woke refreshed. It had been a long time since I had slept so well. Moreover, ever since I had stopped drinking I used to wake up every day without a hangover.

By 12:00 noon and I was having my first bite of sandwich which my mother made for me before leaving for the temple. My father was resting and Joy was reading his course book as his exams were going on.

My phone started ringing. It was almost a week since I heard my mobile ring as I had no colleagues and my friends were all dispersed. Surprisingly it was Arvind from Dubai. I got all excited as it had been many days since we had interacted with each other.

"Hi Nekman? How are you champ? I miss you and Surjeet a lot!"

"We also miss you a lot dude. How everything is at your end? How's your startup doing?"

"All good - you tell how things are at your end?"

I paused at this, then replied, "All is well!"

"Nothing is well Nekman," he said heavily.

"What happened? Isn't everything alright?"

"I should ask you this question Nekman!" I had a hint of what's coming and stayed silent.

"Nekman, don't you consider Surjeet and me as part of your family?"

"Of course…"

"Then why the hell didn't you tell us about uncle's operation? Surjeet also came to know only a day back!"

"I know I should have told you all Arvind, but sometimes situations are such that you yourself are not aware of what you're doing."

"Still Nekman, that's no excuse."

I stayed silent.

"Hey Nekman, leave the past - first tell me how is uncle doing now?"

"He is fine and out of danger."

"Nekman, Surjeet has told me everything - that you have left the job and all that you're going through, I just want to say that if you need any help, Surjeet and I are there for you."

"You don't need to tell me that, I know it brother."

"Yes brother, please take care of yourself," he said and hung up.

After chatting with Arvind, I took a shower, bowed in front of God and prayed for the strength and inspiration to do something good in life.

So now what to do? Yes, this was the question I faced every day as soon as I got out of bed. Last night I had been so motivated by Mr. Pillai's interview that I started thinking about starting up a creative food joint. But not just another food joint - my Idea was to offer more than food.

I took out my laptop and began searching for commercial space nearby where I could reasonably rent a space for my venture. I didn't worry too much about the concept and cuisine as I was fairly confident that I would come up with something.

Searching for a place was not an easy job. I called on many numbers provided on various internet property websites and also registered my number on many property websites so I could get options on good properties at low rates.

A week passed by and I did meet a number of property dealers but didn't achieve anything. Some locations were not good and the good locations were too expensive. In the midst of this process, one day, I got a call from an agent whose name was Mr. Ramanuj.

Mr. Ramanuj asked me to come to his office as he was had some good properties listed, within my budget. Actually my budget was zero, but I planned to borrow some money from market on interest.

To open up a restaurant I would need enough for six months' rent which should not exceed three lakhs - that is fifty thousand rupees per month on an average.

I prepared myself to risk six lakh rupees for six months and if the idea didn't work, I planned to join any job, at least until I could pay back the rupees six lakh plus interest to whoever had loaned me the money.

I was aware that after my dad recovered he would rejoin work again and at least there would be no bread-butter crisis at home. Keeping this in mind I was prepared to take a risk.

On Sunday afternoon I went to visit the real estate dealer, Mr. Ramanuj.

"Excuse me," I said to the receptionist at the front desk, "I have an appointment with Mr. Ramanuj."

"Ok sir, please wait for a moment, let me check," she said.

I sat down on a sofa and looked around. It was large office with beautiful interiors. I had observed two things that differentiated real estate offices from other offices: first, they have very beautiful interior and second, they are open on Sundays and Saturdays for which I pitied the people working in real estate. Half an hour later I was still waiting. I went to the receptionist again to ask for Mr. Ramanuj.

"Oh so sorry sir, he is free now. I forgot to tell you please go straight and then right, the first cabin is Mr. Ramanuj's." I left without a word of thanks – annoyed at her inefficiency.

Mr. Ramanuj was the General Manager of the real estate company.

When I entered his cabin the first thing I saw were leaflets and brochures of different property projects laid out on a table with four landline phones and 3 mobiles.

"Mr. Nekman, I was waiting for you, welcome," he greeted me with a smile. I was happy that everyone in the office was not like the receptionist.

"Mr. Nekman, tell me what you would like to drink?"

"Nothing, thanks," I said.

"No please tell me - will a glass of coke be fine?" he asked me politely.

I agreed and he ordered one from the pantry. We got down to the business at hand.

"Mr. Ramanuj, like I told you over the phone, I need a 3000 sq. ft. space on rent in a good location of Delhi."

"Okay sure, but for what purpose do you need it?"

"I am planning to open a restaurant."

"But this much space will not be sufficient for a restaurant, you should go in for at least 7000 sq. ft. he said.

"No - for two reasons – first, my budget is limited and second, my idea is bit different so I can manage in 3000 sq.ft. to start with. If, by God's grace my business takes off, then I will definitely expand to a bigger area."

"As you say Mr. Nekman, but I tell you we don't do deal with such sizes, at least there should be a requirement of more than 5000 sq. ft. I am very sorry but you have just wasted my precious time."

"Excuse me Mr. Ramanuj, it was you who asked me to meet you. I already told you what my requirement was and now you are insulting me!"

"Mr. Nekman, I'm sorry but I have to ask you to leave. You don't have the money to rent 5000 sq. ft. and you talk about running a restaurant?" he sneered.

In the meanwhile, the glass of coke arrived but he told the pantry boy to take it back. I was badly embarrassed by his comments and lack of hospitality.

"Thank you so much for your precious time Mr. Ramanuj," I said sarcastically.

"You leave now!" he spoke roughly.

"Yes I am leaving, but at least speak politely," I said.

"You need not tell me how to talk, just get out!" He rang for Security, to get me out of the premises.

"No need to call Security, I have my own self-respect. I am leaving. One last thing Mr. Ramanuj, you never know when time takes a turn and things change. One should always be grounded - this is my sincere advice," I said, before leaving his cabin.

"Get out you fucker," he abused me. I slammed his cabin door as I left.

I was totally upset and demoralized after this encounter.

In deep thought I came outside the office building and a sat on a bench. I looked at my watch and wondered when the bad times were going to end. Suddenly I felt a hand on my shoulder, and this time it was no thief's, it was Mr. Black Shirt's.

"Nekman, how come you are here?" Mr. Black Shirt asked me.

"Mr. Black... sorry I mean Mr. Ranjeet, you are out of jail?"

"Yes my boy, I am out and now everything is good."

"Where is your brother?"

"I have sent him out of India for a deal, he will be back soon."

"That's great! I'm happy for you." I beamed at him.

"Well, what you are doing outside this office?"

"Nothing much," I said dejected.

"What happened Nekman? Tell me."

"Nothing... this office is filled with morons!"

"What? Tell me exactly what happened."

I described my humiliating experience with Mr. Ramanuj.

He smiled at the end of it and said: "Come with me."

I was surprised at his reaction and wondered why we were heading back into the building.

I promptly asked him, "Do you know someone in this office?"

"This is my office," he said and I was surprised. I recalled that in jail he had told me that he was running a big business and now apparently, this was the business. He was a big property dealer and consultant.

The moment we entered the building, each and every person sprang to attention, saying: "Good afternoon, sir."

He headed straight for Ramanuj's cabin and made me sit there. Mr. Ramanuj started sweating, seeing me with his boss.

"Mr. Ramanuj," Ranjeet said sternly. "Is this the way to attend to a customer, the way you have attended to Mr. Nekman?"

"No sir, sorry sir," Mr. Ramanuj said.

"Just get out of this office right away before I call Security to throw you out," Mr. Ranjeet told him baldly.

'Sorry sir,' Mr. Ramanuj started crying in front of him and even apologized to me.

"Do you know Nekman is like my younger brother?" When he heard this Mr. Ramanuj squirmed with embarrassment and I felt very good.

"Mr. Ranjeet, please spare him. Don't fire him," I said.

"Okay Nekman, if you say so. I'll not fire Mr. Ramanuj this time - but if you repeat this behavior I will definitely fire you!" Mr. Ranjeet said, glaring at Mr. Ramanuj.

"Please sir, it will never happen again, I am really sorry," Mr. Ramanuj pleaded, now totally humbled.

Mr. Ranjeet then took me to his cabin.

The moment I entered Mr. Ranjeet cabin, my eyes went round, looking at the size of his cabin which was very huge and beautifully done up.

"Mr. Ranjeet, your cabin is just mind blowing!"

"Thanks, Nekman." he said.

He pressed a button and asked for two glasses of coke. Within minutes I had got my glass of coke back! I smiled to myself at the thought. I drank the whole glass of coke – every sip restored the respect I had lost and assuaged the hurt that I'd felt a few minutes before.

"Thank you, Mr. Ranjeet, for the coke."

The Fresh Start

The glass of coke was the turning point and put me on track for fresh start to my life. Mr. Ranjeet offered me a location that was ideal for what I had in mind. In fact he offered me the place free of cost, but I insisted on paying rent for it. After a long time I felt that things were going my way. The opportunity for doing something made me feel very positive.

Two week after the COKE episode, I had secured the space for the restaurant. The only thing left was to start executing my concept, which I knew was most important and critical to its success.

As I've already mentioned, my idea was not just about food it was a lot bigger than that. The first thing I concentrated upon was the color of the walls; I wanted my restaurant to be full of bright colors which would bring positive energy to each and every customer. In addition, I also wanted to have a good number of different and attractive lights to bring hope and brightness into every visitor's life.

"4000 rupees for two containers of color?" I asked the shop keeper where I went to buy wall paint.

"Yes sir, the kind of glossy and neon colors you want are expensive."

Those days neon was very much in so I thought of spreading some neon goodness in my restaurant.

I paid 25,000 rupees for the colors including labor charges for painting, which was to be completed in two weeks.

Once painting was complete, then I went in for lights and, by God's grace, I got a good deal on those.

I took a loan of 6 lakh rupees at 20 % interest, payable in two years. I now had 6 lakhs in my pocket and one year time to make it or lose it.

The interiors, paints and lights cost me a total of Rs. 1.5 lakh. The remaining 4.5 lakhs was the capital I had in hand for running costs, till I broke even and started earning profits.

Everything went on schedule and soon it was only a few days to the opening. I managed to get two people to work as waiters and one person for cleaning but now the main challenge was to find a master chef, that too on a low salary. I was not in a position to pay the chef more than 10,000 rupees per month as per my budget. One thing I was confident of was that whoever joined me as chef would be happy, as my restaurant was all about creative food with a small and innovative menu.

It was 5 pm in the evening and I was going back from my restaurant, in between I felt hungry and stopped at a small road food stall selling rolls.

"Can I have one double chicken egg roll?" I asked the person who was making the rolls.

"Sir, here is your roll, please taste it and tell me how you like it."

I took a bite and found it seriously amazing: "The roll is damn good my friend!" I told the roll maker.

"Thank you sir," he said.

"From where did you learn how to make these rolls?"

"I taught myself in the field sir. Initially I use to make very bad rolls and some of the customers used to shout at me, but slowly and steadily, I became an expert in rolls as well as many other dishes."

"Okay, good for you!"

"Yes sir, now I've been making rolls here for more than four years."

"Great my friend, you're the living proof for the statement: 'Practice makes a man perfect.'"

"Thank you sir," he smiled.

'What is your good name?"

"Roshan, my name is Roshan"

"Thank you Roshan for this wonderful roll," I paid him and left.

That night at dinner, my father asked me: "How is your restaurant coming along?"

"Pretty good dad," I said confidently, tucking into my dinner.

My father was happy seeing me working hard.

"Nekman, why aren't you eating properly?" mom asked me.

"I am not feeling hungry today mom - on my way back I had some delicious rolls."

"Rolls?"

"Yes. They were the most delicious rolls I have ever eaten. I want someone like that roll-guy for my restaurant, who cooks from his heart," I said.

"Surely you will find someone my son," my mom blessed me with a smile.

"Brother why don't you ask this roll-guy to work for you?" Joy suggested.

"Joy he is running his own business, why would he join me for a small salary?"

"Yes, that's true," Joy said.

After dinner I lay on my bed, my mind running through all the things that had to be done. I was ready to work hard but I needed a pinch of luck as well. I said good night and best of luck to myself and slept that night.

I realized one thing, when you are tired after a day of rigorous work, you always get sound sleep at night. That's why our elders advise us to work hard.

It was 1 pm in afternoon, I was busy supervising the labor who were completing work on the interiors.

"Hey, please do it properly!" I shouted at one of the laborers who was fixing the lights on wall. "Where is the carpenter who was doing the wood work just now?"

"Sir he's taking a toilet break," the laborer replied.

"When he comes back, ask him to meet me." I was feeling very positive because I was actually working towards a goal, rather than only dreaming about it.

"Sir, did you call me?" It was the missing carpenter.

"Look, I've already explained to you the kind of furniture I want and I hope you're following instructions. Now there's one more thing I need from you," I said. "I need you to make a wooden platform in the center of our dining area and it should be 3ft in height and approximately 5ft in diameter, I said.

"It can be done sir, but what purpose should it serve?"

"Sure I will tell you, but not right now," I said with a smile on my face.

Another day of hard work came to an end and I started the commute from restaurant to home. This had become my daily routine. My restaurant was almost ready but still I was not able to find the right Chef that I had in mind. My head was throbbing with the start of a headache, I thought

I'd take a diversion and grab one of Roshan's delicious rolls.

After 25 minutes of traffic I reached the junction where Roshan had his shop but there was nothing there.

"Hey excuse me!" I motioned to a guy who was cleaning the street with his big broom, where Roshan's shop used to exist.

"Yes sir?"

"There used to be a shop here. I had rolls from that shop two weeks back. Where it has gone?" I asked him

"Are you are talking about Roshan's shop?"

"Yes, that's the one. Where's Roshan's shop gone?"

"A few days back, due to some political issue, there was an order from the government that all the shops on this street were to be demolished. Some government workers came here and destroyed all the street shops here."

In India, as you know, these shakedowns by the government are quite common, every time there's a new political party.

"Oh shit, that is unfair," I said. "Do you, by any chance, know where Roshan lives?"

"Sir I don't know the exact address but I can tell you the location."

He gave me directions and I set off to find Roshan.

After a good 40 minutes of driving in the heat and dust I finally found his house. It was a small shack in a poor part of town. The roads were narrow, with room for only one car at a time. Luckily I made it without having to accommodate any other automobiles.

After asking around here and there, I finally reached his door and knocked.

The door was open by a young girl of around 11 or 12 years.

"I'm here to meet Roshan. Is he here?"

"Brother is not at home. He has gone to buy milk. He will be back soon," she said with an innocent smile.

"Okay I'll wait."

She looked at me uncertainly for a few minutes then, finally, invited me in.

I went inside the house and realized his sister was his only family and no one else. The house was only as big as a luxury sedan of rich people. There were no walls - only a single space which served as kitchen, dining and bedroom. They probably had to use the public toilets.

"Do you want water?" his sister offered.

"No thanks", I said just as Roshan entered the house.

"Hey Roshan," I shook hands with him.

"Hello sir!" He seemed shocked at finding me in his house.

"I know you must be wondering what I'm doing here."

"Yes sir?"

"Well today I went to your shop and came to know that your shop was demolished by political workers?"

"Yes sir, you are right," he said and the poor fellow started to cry.

"Sir, I have only one sister whom I wanted to educate. But I think that's not possible now. For the past three days, I have not even been able to put food on the table. That shop was the only source of income for me. Now I have no idea what to do!" he wept.

"Okay, first stop crying. See your little sister is watching you and getting upset," I said.

"Yes sir," he said and controlled himself.

"Roshan, now listen to me. I came here to make you an offer, but I don't know whether you will like it or not," I said.

"What offer sir?" he asked puzzled.

"Roshan, I am opening a new restaurant and I'm looking for a chef. I know you have magic in your hands and you cook awesome food, therefore I will be honored if you will work for me."

"Sure sir. I will surely work for you," his eyes lit up with hope.

"Thanks Roshan, but one thing I want to make clear - initially I will not be able to pay you a big salary but, if, by God's grace, the restaurant becomes a hit, then I will give you 10 percent of the profits in addition to your salary."

He looked at me blankly for a fraction of second.

"Roshan? Do you want to accept my offer?"

"Sir, thank you so much!" He hugged me tightly.

That's how I found the kind of Chef I always wanted for my restaurant, who would work, not only for a salary but to satisfy his passion. Roshan had the passion and the talent for creative food, that's what I believed.

Now my restaurant was almost ready and staffing was also complete, about which I was feeling very happy. I began to believe that my good times were starting.

Of course, there was still the question of whether my restaurant would be a hit or not, but on other hand, I was not scared because I had given it my 100 percent. I thought that if, despite all my hard work, my restaurant still failed, then I would try something else, but not give up on life.

Stardom

The one thing which everyone desires in life is love and that's what I planned to give everyone. As I mentioned earlier, opening a restaurant was just a prop for my main concept and my main idea was STARDOM.

STARDOM – the central concept, was all about making everyone feel loved. I named my restaurant 'STARDOM'. Another creative idea was the wooden platform in the center of the restaurant. The idea was to allow people to come to the center, express themselves and receive love and attention from all the others in the restaurant.

The idea was also to provide a unique cuisine for which I had already set the menu with Roshan. Our menu was extremely creative, it included dishes such as: Facebook chat, Google aloo, Laila ka pyaar, Chacha ki rajai and kambal qutai, etc.

The reason behind such creative names was to put a smile on people's faces and make food fun for them. Totally, we offered 5 mains, 5 starters, 2 desserts, 5 non-alcoholic drinks and 5 alcoholic drinks.

People usually find it easier to express themselves after a couple of drinks, so one thing I was clear about, I was definitely going to serve alcohol.

At 8 am, my family and staff assembled together for the opening ceremony at my restaurant. I kept the ceremony simple as money was already running out.

Once the prayer was done, we did a simple inauguration and my mom dad gave me and my staff, loads of blessings.

I was aware that during daytime hours there would be less business and that the main business would take place from 5 pm to 2 am at night. Considering this, I scheduled the restaurant timings as 2 pm-2 am where the staff had to report from 12 noon to 2 am. My personal timings were 24 x 7 as I wanted my idea to be a success.

Everything was in place. It was our first day and I was waiting for people to come and try the restaurant. By 8 pm only two people had come in. No doubt they appreciated the food, but this was not what I expected. I wanted to have a larger audience for earning money and to execute the activities - which were to make everyone lively and express their hearts out.

"Sir, shall we wrap up for today?" Roshan asked.

"Yes," I said in a low voice as there were no diners. We had ended up serving only five customers and it was only 11:00 pm, but I decided to wrap up because I had no hope of anyone coming after 11 pm.

"Take care guys, no need to worry. I think tomorrow will be a great day for us!" I said to my staff.

A month went by and still every day we were serving just 10-15 people. Everything was good and there were no complaints. The customers seemed happy with the food and service, but 10-15 people was not my target.

That night, I was scratching my head wondering how to increase footfalls in my restaurant when suddenly I heard a loud noise from the kitchen.

"What are you doing Joy?" I shouted.

"Nothing brother. I cooked Maggi and was pouring it into a glass bowl which burst from the heat."

"Are you are alright?" I asked.

"Yes I am fine, don't worry," Joy said. "How is your restaurant going?"

"Not that good."

"Why what happened?"

"I really don't know. Everything is good - the colors, the décor the chef, yet footfalls are not increasing. I'm really surprised at that."

"Brother have done any marketing?"

"Yes, of course Joy - I have put up a lot of banners, boards and pamphlets. I have distributed them across all the nearby areas so people can come in."

"Oh, so marketing is your problem!"

"What are you saying?"

"Yes if you will go on marketing this way surely you will remain unsuccessful in increasing your footfalls," Joy said.

"What should I do then?"

"Go digital of course."

"Digital??"

"Yes go for digital marketing. Brother you are in the 21st century. These days internet is spreading like fire. You yourself use so many apps in your daily life like Facebook, YouTube, Google, etc. so how can you rely on only physical marketing to get you footfalls. Go digital brother! Set up a Facebook page, make web banners or make a promotional video and upload it on You Tube. Do a lot of creative things on a digital platform to spread awareness for your restaurant," he finished his speech.

"Yes of course - you are so right Joy!" I said.

I thought about it for a minute.

"Hey Joy, I want you to handle the Digital Marketing for me."

"Me??"

"Yes and don't worry I will talk to mom. You can continue with your studies, I need only two hours daily from you so we can do all this digital stuff, because I know you are very clued in about all these digital gizmos."

Joy was delighted to help. This is how I stepped into the digital world. I realized that I had to be digitally strong to grow business in the market, because that was need of the hour.

Every evening, from 5 pm-7 pm, Joy and I sat down to work on digital marketing activities for the restaurant. We put STARDOM on every possible platform - Facebook, Twitter, Blogs, etc.

We made up some funny slogans, jingles and number of attractive things for awareness around food which we use to upload on our Facebook Page, we also put up an attractive website for the restaurant to create a curiosity in viewers to come to STARDOM. All this got executed because of Joy, otherwise I would never have thought of introducing my restaurant to the digital world.

In twenty days I began to see results. Footfalls to the restaurant increased after all the digital marketing we did.

It was 11:30 pm and my restaurant was almost full - that was the day when I decided to make everyone enjoy stardom. That was the day after which I never looked back.

"Ladies and gentleman, I hope you are enjoying your food and drinks." I jumped onto the wooden platform in middle of the restaurant and shouted loudly to catch everyone's attention.

"Yes," a number of people responded loudly.

"Thank you very much for all the money you are spending in my restaurant," I said.

All shouted: "You are welcome!"

"I think I should give you something more, which can add more value to your experience - because I want each and everyone here, not just to enjoy food, drinks and ambience, but much more!"

"What's that much more?" One guy from the audience who was high on alcohol, stood up and asked.

"STARDOM!" I shouted and everyone was surprised.

"STARDOM is not just the name of my restaurant but an opportunity for all of you to get stardom for a night - when you are in STARDOM. All of you can see I am standing in a wooden circle which is not just a piece of wood but a stage for all of you, where any one of you can come and just do whatever you want to do - except strip tease," I said and everyone laughed.

"Yes, any one of you can come on this stage and can perform whatever you like, for instance you can narrate a story, or dance, or sing, or do mimicry or simply speak your heart out. Also, there is an option for all of you to get your stage performance recorded and uploaded on You Tube - which will be done if you wish." I wound up.

There was silence in the room and everyone stared at me as if was masturbating in front of them.

"Hey man," a small chap who must have been just 5 ft. 1 inch tall and in his early thirties stood up and said, "Can I came over to the stage?"

The whole crowd in the restaurant looked at that little chap in astonishment, wondering what he was up to.

"Yes, sure my brother, come forward," I said into the pin-drop silence.

The little chap slowly walked up and when he reached the stage, he suddenly jumped into the center and said to me, "Please record my video."

"Hey all you beautiful people here tonight, I am really amazed that this guy who is owner of the restaurant has seriously thought of this creative idea where people can deliver whatever they want to.

Well as all of you can see I am a bit short or I must say very short - throughout my life, whether at school, college or office, everywhere I've had to deal with several jokes, but I never got depressed instead I always took everything very light-heartedly. Well that situation has changed now, as I am depressed. Yes! And the reason for my depression is that there is a girl with whom I have fallen in love. For six months I have been trying to express my feelings to her, but my height issue is holding me back – what's worse is she's taller than me.

But today, through this platform, where I can do anything, I would like to propose to that girl. If she doesn't accept my proposal – no worries! I don't mind, but yes I need to express myself now - because the feeling has been building up in me for six months. Today, if I don't express my feelings for her - it will turn into poison!

With her, my life will be a heavenly treat where everything good will be ours. I will look after her till my last breath and promise to stand by her through every good and bad moment of life. She is with me tonight sitting in my group."

After a minute's pause he said," Maria I love you!" The girl rose slowly from her seat.

All were still silent – watching to see whether Maria would accept the little chap's proposal or not.

After two minutes of suspense, the girl ran towards him, jumped on the stage and kissed him. At that moment the whole crowd at the restaurant jumped up and gave them a huge round of applause, accompanied by whistles and hooting.

STARDOM had arrived with a bang. This was exactly what I was looking for. After this my life took another three sixty degree turn but this time, the turn was for the better. I never looked back.

That proposal not only changed life for that couple, but changed mine as well.

Slowly and steadily my restaurant grew famous. People used the platform to perform different things and many of them asked for their performances to be recorded and uploaded onto our FB page. From a business perspective I must say, the internet platform was major a contributor to making my restaurant a viral hit.

That day, I realized that along with destiny, hard work also pays off. There is always a possibility that you will fail a number of times, however hard you work, still you need to get back on your feet and try again - that is the way to live life.

Respect and flow with time. Time is the biggest mentor and teacher in the world.

31

Nekman

"Hello everyone and welcome to our show, ''Nights with Nina''. I'm your host Nina and in today's show, I am interviewing a gentleman who was – once upon a time, a big failure: a person who had his heart broken, who lost his job, became a drunkard, went to jail and even, became a thief.

Please give a huge round of applause to your favorite, charismatic, charming, flamboyant and the winner of this year's award for the fastest billionaire in India's restaurant industry, the one and only - Nekman!"

Yes, it was me.

I became a billionaire. 11 years had passed since the launch of STARDOM. With God's grace, I had successfully opened a chain of STARDOM restaurants on the same theme, and expanded into other hotels as well. Totally, there were 1180 outlets of STARDOM all over the world, and 20 hotels. My name was enough, in the market, to make any restaurant a success.

I never allowed success to change me. I was the same old Nekman, but the only thing that had changed, was that I was a bit more confident.

"Nekman, welcome to our show!" the interviewer greeted me.

"Thank you so much," I said and waited for the applause to come to an end.

I wore a black Armani jacket with a gold Rolex on my wrist.

"Nekman, before starting this interview I would like to tell you, that you are looking damn hot," the interviewer said.

"Thank you so much Nina." I blushed a bit.

"My first question to you is…why STARDOM?"

"Because everyone in this universe wants to feel like a star!"

"Great!" she smiled.

"Is it true that you once became a thief?"

"Yes."

"Do you mind telling us what drove you to it?"

"You seemed to have done your research Nina! I did it for a good cause – the money was to save my father who was in hospital at that time. I knew it was wrong, but yes, it's the truth. I did become a thief thought I was never caught for the deed." Everyone was surprised that I had openly admitted it.

"Moving on…in one of your interviews, you mentioned that you had a depressing love story – can you tell us a bit more about that?" she asked.

"Nothing, but I must say it was the inception for my success," I said.

"Oh, you are a bit precise with your answers!" she said, sarcastically.

"Yes I know," I smiled.

You always wanted to be an actor but did not get the opportunity. Tell us what you still dream to be??

Yes I dream to be and it is always good to dream but I don't thing that it will become a reality someday. If by any chance your dream becomes a reality then celebrate other wise move on.

Coming to my Actor part, I always wanted to be a superstar to be rich and famous which I think I am now, I said with a smile.

Also, Ms. Nina, one thing I forgot to tell you that I have invested in a Big Budget Hollywood movie and the director of the film has asked me to do the second lead in it. Listening to this everyone who were present there got surprised and congratulated me.

"At one point in your life, you became a drunkard. Is that true?"

"Yes, that's absolutely true. I was going through a very bad time and I though then that drinking would make me feel better - but that's not true. I suggest that anyone going through a bad phase like I did, try to fight with your pain without alcohol - if you want to drink, drink in happiness!"

"Hmm… my next question is about when you quit your job – were you afraid of the future?"

"No, because I knew that it was not something that I wanted to do for the rest of my life. When I went into business, I promised myself that even if I failed, I wouldn't stop trying. Even if I earned less, at least I would be happy doing something I really wanted to do.

One more thing, many times in life we are not able to do what we want. There may be a number of reasons why – fear of failure, lack of capital, no opportunity - but that doesn't mean you should stop trying. If there's no opportunity, create your own. Keep moving and keep exploring.

If you doesn't succeed in one goal then surely some other goal is waiting for you. Another important thing I would like you to remember - never look back at your history but look to the future. The future belongs to those who look forward – this is what life has taught me."

"Well, thank you for those powerful words and for sharing your experiences. I'm sure our young entrepreneurs will find them inspiring," Nina smiled.

"Thank you!"

"One last question, Nekman," she said.

"Yes?"

"One word which describes you the most?"

"Unstoppable."

"Awesome!"

"I have a request for you, Nina."

"Yes tell me, Nekman."

"I want you to invite my parents on stage."

"Sure!" My mum and dad were invited on the stage.

The only thing my parents said was: "We are proud to have him as our son." My tears rolled freely because only I knew what a long journey it had been. I hugged my parents tightly.

So this is my story. There is a Nekman in everyone one of you. Life is not a straight road - life is a road full of twist and turns, with many speed breakers, red lights, potholes... it's only by crossing all these hurdles that one becomes a good driver.

So don't curse the difficulties of life, accept them as challenges, and became a good driver.

All the best.

LIVE, LAUGH, EXPLORE and BE UNSTOPPABLE!

Afterword

You may be wondering what happened to many of the characters in my story, since you met them 11 years ago:

Hinsa: As I had promised myself, I returned her money. One day, five years after STARDOM turned successful, I sent one of my employees to her house with the money, five times the amount that I had stolen from her - with a name slip, "Nekman".

Joy: He became Head of Marketing for all my ventures and my partner in business.

Surjeet and Arvind: Both stayed in touch with me and are also shareholders in many of my outlets. Through the years they always stood by me, and I by them.

Silvana: Silvana and I married each other seven years after STARDOM was launched. Mom was upset that she was not an Indian, but has come to love her.

Mr. Ranjeet: He played a major role in my success and he was too a shareholder in many of my ventures.

Roshan: He became the Head Chef of all my restaurants and ten years later performed his sister's wedding grandly.

Mrs. Marwah: One fine day, when STARDOM was well on its way, she called me and said that it had taken her five year's but she had finally taken my advice and got a divorce. I was happy for her and invited her to be an investment consultant for STARDOM restaurants. Now she too is a part of my business family.

LIVE, LAUGH, EXPLORE and BE UNSTOPPABLE!

About the Author

Nishant Nalwa has done his MBA from Amity Business School and is currently working in the Indian IT industry. He lives with his parents and his wife Swarnali Nalwa, who also works in the IT sector.

Nishant always wanted to do something creative in his life but destiny had other plans and he landed up living the corporate life. His transformation into a writer came about because his 9-6 job frustrated him. He was able to fulfill his creative need through writing.

Hence, he became a writer..

www.ingramcontent.com/pod-product-compliance
Lightning Source LLC
Chambersburg PA
CBHW051343020726
47501CB00007B/2236